Mystery Loves Company

A Myrtle Clover Cozy Mystery, Volume 25

Elizabeth Spann Craig

Published by Elizabeth Spann Craig, 2024.

This is a work of fiction. Similarities to real people, places, or events are entirely coincidental.

MYSTERY LOVES COMPANY

First edition. September 17, 2024.

Written by Elizabeth Spann Craig.

For Cassie and Rebecca, with thanks for their help
with subplots!

Chapter One

"**M**y baseboards are a disgrace, Puddin. This must be rectified immediately."

Puddin, Myrtle Clover's housekeeper, wrinkled her nose. This did nothing to improve her general appearance. She sported an unhappy expression on her pudgy, pasty face. "You know I don't like it when you don't talk English."

"It's the king's English."

Puddin sniffed. "Didn't think we had kings over here."

"You're prevaricating. Stalling. The point is, these baseboards must be cleaned immediately. They're positively frightful."

Puddin studied the offending baseboards. "They're kinda low to the floor."

"That's their nature," said Myrtle through gritted teeth.

"My back is thrown." This was said in a rather proud way. Puddin likely believed her back had come through for her in her hour of need by helping her avoid meaningless grunt work.

Myrtle was tiring of the conversation. She didn't understand why she should have to motivate her housekeeper to keep house. But considering she was a retired schoolteacher and very much on a budget, she didn't have the option to search for better help. Other housekeepers were far, far out of her league. But Puddin may not be keenly aware of her financial situation, and she did know one way to motivate her.

"It's a pity your back is so acrobatic," said Myrtle acerbically. "I suppose I'll have to call your cousin Bitsy up and have her run by to take care of the baseboards."

Puddin did appear to have her back up now, thrown or not. "Bitsy?" she asked scornfully. "She's expensive."

"Sadly, yes. But she is reputed to do a truly excellent job. And it appears I have no choice. Because of my advanced years, I'm unable to clean them myself."

Puddin heaved a sigh, casting a resentful eye at the baseboards. "Reckon I can clean 'em," she muttered grimly.

"That's the spirit! Just think about how much better they'll look."

Puddin said, "Don't know why they have them things anyway."

"Baseboards? I suppose to keep the walls from being scuffed by vacuums. And perhaps as a decorative touch. I don't really care what their purpose in life is, only that they look a lot better than they do right now."

Puddin threw out what must have been her ace in the hole. "It's Valentine's Day, Miz Myrtle."

"And the baseboards will love you for making them so sparkly."

There was a light tap at Myrtle's front door. Puddin looked toward it with interest and a bit of hope. Thinking there might be an excellent way to stall on the other side of that door.

Miles was on her doorstep. He looked a little startled when he saw his friend. Her face was flushed and her white poof of hair stood up like Einstein's. "Is everything okay over here?"

"Sadly, no. Puddin has once again been resistant to cleaning. I've been doing a lot of bending over to demonstrate the filthiness of my baseboards." Myrtle gestured Miles to come inside.

Miles mused, "Does anyone really notice baseboards?"

Puddin hollered, "That's what I said!"

Myrtle said coldly, "*I* do. I notice baseboards. While I was sitting in my chair, they were leering at me."

Miles and Myrtle took a seat. Puddin looked as if she might join them for a minute before Myrtle gave her a frigid look. Puddin walked off, muttering darkly to herself.

"You see the type of foolishness I have to put up with," said Myrtle, gesturing toward the recalcitrant Puddin. "It's complete nonsense over here at all times."

"It sounds like her insurrection is over."

Myrtle sniffed. "For today, maybe. Unfortunately, we'll have to go through the same charade when she comes back out here in a couple of weeks. It's intolerable. But let's chat about other things. I feel my blood pressure starting to creep up, and my blood pressure is always perfectly behaved."

Miles said in an offhand manner, "In other matters, I see you went viral."

"What? I certainly have not. I'm completely healthy. The very idea."

Miles said, "I meant that your social media post went viral. That many people viewed and shared it."

Myrtle looked a bit shifty. "I have no idea what you're talking about."

"I believe you do. You have a recurring post on social media called 'Daily Absurdities in the Paper.' It tracks typos printed in the *Bradley Bugle*."

Myrtle said sharply, "Not typos. Grammatical errors."

"So you admit to being the brains behind it."

"Not a bit," said Myrtle. "I only know that if mistakes were pointed out in our local newspaper, they wouldn't be typos at all. They'd be flagrant grammatical errors of the worst possible kind."

"The avatar for the anonymous social media account is a tree."

Myrtle sniffed. "Then it's inexplicable that you would connect such a thing with me."

"'A crepe *myrtle* tree.'"

Myrtle scowled. "I believe they're considered shrubs, not trees."

"That's beside the point, isn't it? And you should be pleased that your post reached so many people. That was your goal, wasn't it?"

Myrtle abruptly decided to drop the entire charade. "No, it wasn't my goal at all. My goal was to find a way to redirect my irritation over the constant errors in the newspaper. From a former student, no less! The scheme worked to a certain degree. Now, let's once again think of another topic. There must be some subject of conversation that won't annoy me."

Miles nodded, but his mind was clearly elsewhere. "Are you busy today?"

"What makes you think I might be busy? You know what my life is like. If it's not book club or garden club day, I likely have nothing to do but stare at my baseboards."

Miles said, "I just thought, since it was Valentine's Day, that there might be a party at Jack's preschool with cupcakes or something."

Jack was Myrtle's grandson and the apple of her eye. "No," she said, "I haven't heard anything about a party. But there *is* something I needed to remember about Valentine's Day. I just can't seem to put my finger on it." Her frown deepened. "Oh no. It's a catastrophe. I forgot something."

"Something at the preschool?"

"Nothing that fun," said Myrtle. "I was supposed to write some soppy feature on Teddy Hartfield, the florist, for the paper. Sloan threw it out at me as an assignment and then didn't mention it again. For heaven's sake."

"The article was supposed to run in today's paper?"

"Yes, yes. Today. That's Sloan's idea of a Valentine's piece . . . interviewing the local florist." She thought for a few moments. "I could change it up, though. Instead of something focused on Teddy, I'll write about how busy a florist is for Valentine's Day. That sounds like a much more interesting story, anyway."

Miles said in a thoughtful tone, "I'm actually acquainted with Teddy."

"I didn't realize you made a point of hanging out at the flower shop."

"I don't," said Miles. "But Teddy plays chess with me."

Miles was part of a local chess club that met to play and engage in the occasional tournament. It was one of those clubs composed mainly of men, a few intrepid women, and a brainy ten-year-old boy with a talent for the game.

"If you know Teddy, that's absolutely perfect. You can accompany me. Perhaps that will make Teddy relax more for our interview."

Miles looked like he might balk. "If we think Teddy is swamped today, it would be better if we didn't bother him. He's probably frantically putting together last-minute orders and delivering them."

"Nonsense. He'll be glad for the free publicity."

Miles frowned. "As far as I'm aware, he shouldn't need it. He's the only florist in town, right? Since Lillian Johnson came to an unfortunate demise, I mean."

Lillian had gotten herself murdered some time ago, and her daughter nor her son had no inclination to run the shop after she died.

"That's true, but having a feature story will remind people they need to buy flowers from time to time. Some people might not think of flowers at all. When they think of gift-giving, their minds might automatically go to sweets or small gifts. Teddy will surely appreciate the reminder that he's there to help them in their hour of need." Myrtle looked at her watch. "The only issue is I'm not altogether sure that I can leave Puddin alone, unsupervised."

Puddin, unrepentantly listening in, snorted loudly. "I'll do a better job without you breathin' down my neck."

Myrtle pursed her lips. "I suppose we can give it a try. Let's head out, Miles."

Miles walked reluctantly to the door, still likely trying to formulate excuses for why they shouldn't visit Teddy on such a busy day. But he couldn't think up any before they reached his car.

At some point along the drive, Miles appeared to be feeling glum. Myrtle decided to ignore his moodiness, instead chatting brightly about Elaine's latest hobby. Her daughter-in-law was a wonderful person and the mother of her equally wonderful grandson. However, when it came to Elaine's attempts to entertain herself with various hobbies, she was an unmitigated disaster.

Myrtle said, "I wanted to give you a heads-up on Elaine's latest craze, because it could end up directly impacting you."

"That's ominous," said Miles, snapping out of his brooding.

"It is. She's baking bread."

Miles said, "Bread baking actually sounds rather pleasant. And somewhat harmless."

"Although Elaine has successfully produced excellent bread in the past, she apparently became over-confident and started experimenting. You should see the bread. I don't know how, but she makes it hard as a rock. You could chip teeth on it. Or lose teeth altogether. She's sure to bring you by a loaf. Remember, I warned you."

It wasn't a long drive to Blossom Serenade, which was situated on the far side of downtown Bradley from Myrtle's house. It was a converted house with a large bay window at the front holding window boxes filled with bright daylilies and ivy climbing the brick walls. It was in an older residential area with ranch houses and children playing in the front yards.

Miles and Myrtle walked up the stone-paved path to the front door of Blossom Serenade. Miles held the door open for her as they stepped inside, a brass bell jingling merrily to announce their entrance. The wooden floor creaked under their feet, but the creaking and the bell were the only sounds Myrtle heard. "Teddy?" she called out. "Teddy, it's Myrtle Clover."

It was very quiet. Creepily quiet, considering the day.

"Maybe he's out delivering flowers," suggested Miles.

"But his van was out front. And he didn't lock the door."

They walked down a narrow hall to a bright room overlooking the backyard. There was an antique wooden counter displaying delicate vases, vintage gardening books, and a brass cash register.

"Teddy!" called Myrtle again, this time louder.

Then Myrtle walked around the counter to look behind it. There, she finally found Teddy. But there was clearly not going to be an interview with him, as he was quite dead.

Chapter Two

Miles quickly joined Myrtle around the counter. He gazed, horrified, at the floor. "Is he gone?"

"I'm afraid so. I did check for a pulse, but there wasn't one. Could you call Red for me?" Red was Myrtle's son and the chief of police. He was also the chief irritant in her life, always wanting to keep her from doing anything remotely interesting. Like investigating mysterious deaths.

While Miles was on the phone with Red, who, from what she could gather, did not sound at all pleased that his mother had discovered another body, she glanced around the crime scene, being very careful not to touch anything. For it was indeed a crime scene, from what Myrtle could see.

Teddy's head rested at an awkward angle, and even from a respectful distance, Myrtle could see the telltale signs of a nasty bump. "Blunt force trauma," she murmured to herself, her years of amateur sleuthing kicking in. It seemed the gentle giant had been felled by a single, powerful blow.

Given Teddy's impressive stature—he had towered over most in town at well over six feet—Myrtle couldn't help but wonder how someone had gotten the drop on him. He wasn't a man easily surprised or overpowered. Whoever had done this must have caught him completely unawares.

As she stood there, careful not to disturb anything, Myrtle's mind was already whirring with questions. Who would want to harm the affable Teddy? And how had they overpowered such a strapping fellow? One thing was certain, this peaceful town had just become the setting for another most troubling mystery. And Myrtle couldn't wait to solve it.

She glanced away, looking for more potential clues. To Myrtle's dismay, a loaf of very hard-looking bread lay nearby.

Miles wrapped up the phone call. "Red's on his way. I bet we'll be able to hear sirens momentarily." Which is precisely when they started.

"See that?" asked Myrtle.

"What? The bread? Maybe Teddy had just returned from grocery shopping."

Myrtle said, "No, that's one of Elaine's signature loaves. You can tell from the way it resembles a baseball bat."

Miles frowned. "Surely, you don't think—"

"No, of course not. Elaine would never murder anyone. Not intentionally, anyway. She's come rather close with one or two of her hobbies. But it certainly looks as if she must have been here."

Miles said, "Did someone use her loaf to kill Teddy?"

"Well, that's going to be up to Red or the state police to determine. But I doubt it. I believe the murder weapon was the heavy vase next to Teddy. At least, I hope that was the case." The siren grew closer.

"I can't imagine who would murder Teddy," said Miles, frowning. "He was such a great guy. Everyone loved being around him."

"Yes, people often say things like that when someone dies unexpectedly. 'He'd give you the shirt off his back,' or 'she had a heart of gold.' Everyone is kind, generous, angelic, and a pillar of the community. But it's rarely one-hundred percent true, is it? People are complex. Perhaps you can mull on things a bit and think about who might not have liked Teddy as much as you did."

Miles offered, "Maybe someone was trying to rob the shop? After all, it's Valentine's Day. We were just saying how Blossom Serenade would be sure to have a high volume of sales today."

Myrtle thought little of this idea, although she knew why Miles would have wanted to glom onto it. He clearly didn't like the idea of his chess friend being murdered. According to Miles's way of thinking, Teddy was above reproach. "The problem with that theory is, the cash register isn't open. I don't believe a thief would leave without getting what they came for."

Conversation quickly became impossible when the siren blasted from directly in front of the shop. Soon a car door slammed, and Red appeared in the doorway, looking hot and bothered on the February day.

"Mama!" he called out.

"Back here," she answered. "Miles and I are near the cash register."

Red hurried into the room. "Okay, I need you two to head outside. Don't touch anything on the way out. I'll join you outside in a minute."

"Teddy is behind the counter," said Myrtle helpfully.

Red muttered something under his breath as Myrtle sailed outside.

Miles's mood had changed from gloomy to fretful as he stared at the florist shop. Myrtle decided not to share with him how the story she was going to be writing for the paper had suddenly gone from page four feature to front page news. It wasn't every day that a murder occurred in the small town of Bradley. Although they happened far more regularly than anyone would perhaps expect. There had been quite a few murdered bodies in what seemed like an otherwise peaceful hamlet. Myrtle had discovered many of them.

Red came out of the shop looking grim and talking on the phone. Then he strode to his cruiser and pulled out crime scene tape to rope off the area. Finally, he joined Myrtle and Miles near Miles's car.

"Okay," he said in an irritated voice. "Let's run through this from the top. What were you two doing here?"

"Are we suspects?" asked Myrtle brightly. It would certainly liven up what had been a very tiresome February.

"No. But I don't know how you have this eerie ability to show up at crime scenes all the time. If you were anyone else but my mother, I'd certainly be investigating."

Myrtle seemed pleased by the idea.

"From the top," repeated Red.

Miles cleared his throat, not wanting to be told a third time. "Well, Myrtle had an assignment to write for Sloan. The article was supposed to be a feature on Teddy Hartfield, but she neglected to do it."

Myrtle was very sensitive about any episode of forgetfulness, thinking Red would use it against her as an excuse to lock her away in Greener Pastures Retirement Home, a prison for the elderly that squatted on the outskirts of Bradley. It boasted state-of-the-art amenities if your definition of state-of-the-art hadn't been updated since the early 1980s. The brochure, which Red often found reason to leave in a prominent location on her coffee table, promised "engaging activities," which Myrtle suspected meant bingo tournaments where the grand prize was an extra cup of tapioca pudding. It also touted "round-the-clock care," which she translated as "someone to remind you to take your pills and make sure you're in bed by 8 PM." "I simply overlooked it because it was such a puerile assignment."

Red tilted his head to one side. "Puerile meaning inconsequential?"

"Trivial. Anyway, it was going to be a piece that ran on Valentine's Day. Sloan never reminded me about it. I decided to run a different kind of story, one about what Valentine's Day is like for a florist. I thought that would make a far more entertaining article."

Red frowned. "You were planning on interviewing Teddy on his busiest day of the year."

"I'm positive he was going to be delighted about the exposure. Why wouldn't he be? Most of the town subscribes to the newspaper, and it would be free advertising for him. Unfortunately, Teddy was sadly unavailable for the interview."

Red sighed. "I'll say. So you entered the shop, couldn't find him, and then looked behind the counter? What did you touch?"

"Well, I had to make sure Teddy didn't simply need an ambulance, although that seemed rather unlikely, looking at him. I felt for an absent pulse. But no, to answer your implied question, Miles and I did not corrupt your crime scene."

Red nodded, looking just as glum as Miles had earlier. "Okay. You two can go head back home. The state police are on their way."

"Lieutenant Perkins?" Myrtle loved Perkins, whom she'd known from quite a few previous investigations.

"Yes, Perkins is coming. But he has a job to do, Mama, so leave him alone, okay?" With that, Red strode back into the shop.

Miles said, "We should leave, Myrtle. Otherwise, we'll be in the way here. And Red won't be happy about that."

"Red isn't happy about anything I do," said Myrtle tartly. "But I suppose we could go back to the house. I should check to see if Puddin is cleaning my baseboards or lounging on the sofa watching morning game shows. I strongly suspect the latter."

They were about to climb into Miles's car when a man called out to them. He was a sturdy man in his forties with graying temples.

"Do we know him?" murmured Miles.

"I do. I taught him English. I'm not sure how much of it stuck, however. He wasn't much of an academic, but he can do anything that's mechanical." Myrtle smiled at the man as he came up.

"Why Curtis Walsh," she said. "How nice to see you."

"How are you, Miss Myrtle?"

Myrtle said, "Well, I'm doing pretty well, aside from a dreadful shock this morning."

Miles gave her a skeptical look at the "dreadful shock" part. Myrtle had been as cool as a cucumber.

Curtis nodded. "I was just coming over to see what's going on at Blossom Serenade. I saw Red's car and then the crime scene tape. I thought I should check it out. Do you know what's happening? Is Teddy okay?"

"Unfortunately, it appears as though Teddy Hartfield might have been murdered."

Curtis's eyes widened. "You're kidding."

"Certainly not."

Curtis quickly amended his statement. "No, of course you're not kidding. But wow, this is a shock." He pointed to a small, well-maintained house next door with a swing set in the side yard. "That's my house right there. You can see why I'm worried."

"I'm sure you're still in a very safe neighborhood. This was more than likely something personal, wouldn't you think? It didn't appear as if the shop had been robbed."

Curtis looked a bit more relieved at this. "Gotcha. Yeah, that makes sense." He was staring at Blossom Serenade, shaking his head. "I can't believe it, though. I wonder what's going to happen to the shop now."

Myrtle asked, "What kind of neighbor was Teddy? Did he live on the premises as well as work here?"

"He did. So it was a hybrid kind of place—both commercial and residential." He grimaced. "I didn't think much of having a commercial property next door to me. Everything else on the street is residential. I mean, my kids play outside and these big delivery trucks were always flying up and down the road. One day there were a couple of trucks outside the shop and one of them blocked my driveway."

"That would have been very irritating," offered Miles.

Curtis looked at Miles curiously, and Myrtle introduced them. "Miles is my friend and neighbor. Miles, this is Curtis Walsh, a former student of mine. I taught him high school English."

Curtis shook Miles's hand. "Yep, she gave it her best shot, but then I ended up going into the construction industry."

"You still need good English in construction," said Myrtle reprovingly. "It makes you look more professional in emails, contracts, and reports. And clear communication is always important for project details to avoid misunderstandings and mistakes."

Curtis grinned at her. "Yes, ma'am. You're absolutely right. I do try my best."

Myrtle said, "I must say that I'm surprised you decided on the construction industry. I'd have thought you'd have gone into automotive repair. You did such a fine job fixing my car the day it died in the teacher's parking lot at the school."

Curtis grinned at her. "You thought you were going to have to sleep at the high school that day. I couldn't let that happen to you. It wasn't a tough repair."

Myrtle said, "It was still very impressive." She paused. "You were saying how annoying it was to have a shop next door."

"Oh yeah. Anyway, like I was saying, there were problems with trucks. Plus, it was just sort of noisy, altogether."

"A floral shop was noisy?" Miles seemed doubtful at this.

"You wouldn't think it, would you? You'd imagine that it would be super-quiet in there. But I think Teddy must have had one of those artistic personalities. He'd be arguing with people all the time."

Myrtle's ears pricked up at this. "Really? With whom did he argue?"

Curtis grinned at her. "Look at you, using correct English like that! I can't get the hang of it. See, that's why I couldn't do good in your class."

"Do well."

Curtis tilted his head to one side. "You thought I did well?"

"No. I mean . . . never mind. You were saying Teddy argued with people," said Myrtle.

"That's right. I guess he wanted everything to be perfect, because if it wasn't, he'd be chewing somebody out. And sometimes, he'd stand outside on the phone, yelling at people. Not sure if those were business calls or what, but they were loud." Curtis glanced over at Blossom Serenade again and said, "Well, I suppose I should be heading out."

Myrtle followed his gaze and saw Red coming down the front walk toward them. Red called out, "Curtis!"

Curtis reluctantly turned back around. Red strode up. "Since you live right next door, I'd like to talk to you for a minute," he said.

Myrtle found it very interesting that Red knew where Curtis lived. Bradley, North Carolina was indeed a small town, but there were hundreds of people in it. Red couldn't possibly know where *everyone* lived. She also knew Curtis and Red weren't good friends, although they'd been in school at roughly the same time. This led her to believe Red knew Curtis lived next door because he'd had some sort of police-related trouble with him in the past.

"What's up, Red?" Curtis asked. There was already a somewhat defensive tone in his voice.

"I know you and Teddy had issues with each other. I'm just covering my bases, you understand. Where were you today?"

Curtis backed up a step. "You're not thinking I hurt Teddy?"

"I'm not thinking anything. I'm just following procedure. The fact of the matter is, you'd call me up to report issues with delivery trucks and customers parking on your property. Like I said, I need to know where you were today."

Curtis frowned. "I've been home today. I didn't have a contracting job yesterday or today. But I haven't taken a step onto Teddy's property, and that's the truth, Red. You can't think I had anything to do with his murder."

Red gave his mother an irritated look at having given Curtis that information. She shrugged. Word was going to spread soon enough, anyway.

"Did you see or hear anything unusual over there?"

Curtis snorted. "The whole day has been unusual over there, in terms of customers. It's Valentine's Day, you know. Busy. I don't know how somebody had the gumption to take Teddy out when so many people were going in and out over there."

At that moment, a couple of police vehicles drove up. Myrtle recognized them as state police cars. Red said, "Okay, Curtis. You're going to be around later? In case I have more questions for you?"

"Sure," said Curtis, sounding less than delighted.

Red walked away to speak with the state police. Curtis watched him go. "Cops always make mountains out of mole-hills," he muttered.

Myrtle hardly thought murder qualified as a molehill. Curtis must have read her mind, because he quickly said, "I mean me being at home all day. And calling in a couple of complaints."

Miles cleared his throat. "I'd imagine it would be very aggravating having customers park on your property. It looks like you have a nice lawn."

From time to time, Miles was an exceptional sidekick, mused Myrtle. This was one of those times. It had looked for a moment as if Curtis was going to stalk back to his house. But he'd clearly re-engaged him.

"Yeah, I put a lot of time into that yard. My kids and their friends play there, so I like to keep things tidy and safe. When customers and trucks are parking in my yard, that doesn't feel safe to me." He stared with irritation toward Red and the state police. "Teddy and I got along fine, no matter what Red says. I did call Red a couple of times to complain, but that's as far as I took things. Red had a conversation with Teddy, and Teddy came over to apologize to me in person. I respected that."

Myrtle said, "Of course, I suppose he wouldn't have had much control over where his customers were parking."

"True. It just aggravated me that his business was bringing people in like that. I wasn't happy when he set up shop here. I wanted the house to stay residential. But Teddy and I talked all the time. I'd ask him how to take care of different plants in my yard. And he helped save a tree that was doing poorly. Any kind of disagreements we had were minor and got taken care of."

Miles said, "Wasn't Teddy involved in local politics?" Curtis gave him a curious look, and he continued. "He and I used to play chess together."

"Sorry for your loss. Yeah, Teddy was involved in . . . well, I guess it was activism. He was real into environmental causes—stuff like that. I'm kind of on the other side of the issue, since I'm a contractor and work a lot with developers. But I could see his point. He cared about living things, right? That made sense, since he was a florist and was handling plants all the time. I just know that endangered animal he was trying to save blocked a planned development."

"What kind of animal was it?" asked Miles curiously.

Myrtle frowned. "I seem to remember reading something about it in the newspaper. A salamander, was it?"

"That's right. They were in a stream that ran right through the property that was going to be developed."

Miles said slowly, "Is development a successful industry in Bradley? I don't seem to see very much of it."

"People find a way of blocking it here," said Curtis. "Nobody wants it in their backyard. But yeah, development makes money when it isn't blocked. We have a nice lake here, after all. People like living here. The town is a draw."

Myrtle said, "That's interesting about Teddy. I didn't realize he was active politically." She looked over at Curtis's yard, where he'd planted some immature Leyland cypresses. They were the type of fast-growing trees a homeowner might plant for privacy. "It looks like you were concerned about privacy issues, too."

Curtis glanced at the trees. "Well, sure. I could just be sitting out in the yard with my wife and kids and all kinds of people would drive up. Mostly guys who'd screwed up and needed to buy last-minute flowers for the wife. But I don't really like being on full display." His face darkened. "We did have more privacy a few weeks ago. But Teddy cut back a ton of shrubbery and some invasive plants on the border of his property. It meant there was no privacy from that side at all."

"Did you talk to him about it?" asked Myrtle.

"Sure, but what could I do? The stuff was on his property. Teddy went off on a spiel about how native plants were so much better than the invasive ones. I felt like he wasn't really listening to me." Curtis raised his hands. "Now, don't be getting suspicious of me, Miss Myrtle. Just because Teddy aggravated me, it doesn't mean I didn't like the guy."

"What was your opinion of him?" asked Myrtle.

Curtis looked momentarily thoughtful. "Maybe Miles can offer his opinion, too. I wonder if we think the same thing. I thought he was a good guy, pretty friendly, talented, and smart. But I also thought it was his way or the highway. Know what I mean?"

Miles nodded. "Teddy liked getting his way."

"Right. And that's not necessarily a bad thing. But it could rub people the wrong way."

Myrtle said, "Do you know if Teddy *really* rubbed someone the wrong way? As in, maybe they'd want to eliminate him?"

Curtis quirked an eyebrow. You could tell he was wondering if his old English teacher was merely being nosy, or whether she was trying to take over the investigation from her police chief son. But he answered immediately. "That's easy. Nat Drake."

Myrtle frowned. "I'm not sure I know him."

"You might not run in the same circles. He's a property developer. Actually, he's the developer on the project I was telling you about. The one that got canceled because of a slug."

It wasn't a slug, but Myrtle decided not to defend the endangered creature to her former student. "I see. So he's angry that the development didn't move forward and he lost income."

"It was really even worse than that. You see, Nat *owns* the property that now can't be developed. So he lost out as both an owner and a developer. He's furious over it. I mean, he's one of those kinds of guys where nothing really seems to touch him usually. I've never seen him show much emotion, and I've known him a long time. He's a good man, but I know he's got a temper. He just doesn't show it. But I can see it in his eyes. His blood pressure has got to be sky high."

"I was wondering when I was in the shop where Teddy's employee was. Ollie Spearman—does he still work here with Teddy?"

Curtis said, "Well, he did until a couple of weeks ago. Something happened, though—Ollie hasn't been around. I've seen him out in town, but not over at Blossom Serenade.

Curtis's phone rang, and he glanced at the name of the caller. "I better go—this is work."

As he headed off, Miles spotted Red glowering at them. "I believe Red wants us to leave the premises."

Myrtle looked over at her son and blew him a big kiss. This did not appear to improve his mood one iota.

"All right, I guess we have enough information for now. Let's run by the *Bugle* on the way home. I need to tell Sloan about my scoop, and that will save me a phone call."

Chapter Three

Miles seemed gloomy again, though, as they set off down the road. Perhaps more distraction was in order prior to the errand to the *Bradley Bugle*. Myrtle said, "Let's drive past Ollie Spearman's place. Teddy's former employee."

"We don't know he's a former employee."

"Curtis says he hasn't been there for weeks. It certainly seems like a reasonable explanation."

Miles's forehead wrinkled. "We're not going to tell Ollie that Teddy died, are we?" Miles was rather squeamish about making these sorts of notifications. One never knew how someone would react.

"What? No, no. We're merely going to do a drive-by."

Miles's forehead was now even more deeply furrowed. "A drive-by *shooting*?"

"Mercy! No, Miles. When have we ever done that? We're not Bonnie and Clyde. For heaven's sake. I'm simply interested in finding out if Ollie is at home. Maybe he's been out murdering Teddy."

Miles said slowly, "I'm not certain that Ollie being out of the house is a sign of guilt. There are many reasons why he might be out. It's Valentine's Day, after all. Maybe he's out getting a greeting card for a special friend."

Myrtle noted with alarm that Miles appeared to be heading directly for the doldrums again. Had someone won his heart? It was most irritating. She needed her sidekick to be sharp, not mooning over some silly filly.

"He lives just down this street. No, over there. Yes, this turn. Watch out for that squirrel!"

Miles muttered, "The squirrel is on the other side of the street."

"Squirrels are notoriously capricious. He or she could easily have decided to dive under your tires. Let's not leave more death in our wakes today."

Miles carefully drove down Ollie's street until Myrtle directed him to park across the street from Ollie's house. It was a pleasant house, with a vibrant yard, despite it being winter.

"Are we surveilling his house now?" asked Miles, looking uncomfortable.

"We're just admiring it. That's our story, if he were to come out and see us."

Miles raised a skeptical eyebrow. "We were so impressed with Ollie Spearman's February yard that we pulled over to the side of the road to stare at it."

"Correct. That's our cover story." Myrtle studied the driveway. "I don't see a car."

"There's a garage," pointed out Miles.

Myrtle sniffed. "No one uses their garages for parking cars. They all function as warehouses for the stuff people should give away, but don't. No, I think Ollie is out and about."

"I suppose he must be setting up shop in his home? After all, presumably he's without income right now. It would be helpful for him to create floral arrangements at home."

Myrtle nodded. "That makes sense. Although he has that hideous pair of muddy boots right there on his front porch. I'd imagine that to be rather off-putting to potential customers."

Miles appeared to be tiring of the short surveillance. "We've seen everything we can see from the road, Myrtle."

Myrtle beamed at him. "You're absolutely right. We should get out of the car and knock on his door. That way, we could be completely sure Ollie is really out of the house."

But Miles was already driving slowly away before Myrtle had the chance to open the car door. "I think that's enough for right now. Let's head over to the *Bugle*."

Miles delved deep in his thoughts during the short drive. Myrtle supposed he must be upset about Teddy's death. "I'm sorry about your friend," she said in what she fondly considered a concerned tone. It might have sounded more curious than concerned.

"What was that?" asked Miles.

"Your friend. The one you're brooding over right now." At least, she hoped he was brooding over his fallen chess club friend and not some woman. The last time he'd been involved in a relationship, it created all sorts of complications.

But Miles didn't appear to recognize the fact that he'd been sad over Teddy. "Ah. That's right. Yes, I feel bad about that. He was a fine chess player."

"He was a good player?"

"Well, he beat me at chess quite a few times," said Miles.

Myrtle wasn't sure that was indicative of any special talent on Teddy's end. After all, *she'd* beaten Miles at chess quite a few times, and she didn't even know the names of all the pieces.

"What was Teddy like? Curtis didn't paint the best picture of him. It sounds like he was loud, argumentative, and liked things to go his way."

Miles considered this. "That's true, actually. But that's not all of who Teddy was. He had a good sense of humor. He seemed kind most of the time. And he had a keen head for business. I remember he mentioned wanting to expand the shop into something of a franchise."

"A franchise? In Bradley?"

Miles said, "No, I think we decided Bradley couldn't handle more than one florist. He wanted to open Blossom Serenade in nearby towns and have them run by staff."

"That was very ambitious of him."

"Yes, it was," said Miles. "It's a real pity he's gone."

Miles parked the car directly in front of the *Bradley Bugle* office in downtown Dappled Hills. Myrtle was supposed to be a mere columnist at the *Bugle*, but was wretchedly unhappy stuck in her role as a helpful hints columnist. Sadly, the helpful hints column was extremely popular, and Sloan, the editor, would likely never let her stop the column. It was bearable, however, as long as she could work as a crime reporter whenever the inevitable murder would happen. You'd never think tiny Bradley, North Carolina would be a hotbed for homicide, but it seemed as if bodies dropped all the time there.

Myrtle had taught Sloan English, as well. She'd taught for so long since the death of her husband that she'd taught everyone in Bradley of a certain age. Sloan had never recovered from being her student and would jump half a mile whenever she entered the door. It was most entertaining.

Sure enough, as soon as Myrtle and Miles walked into the *Bugle* office, Sloan nearly fell out of his swivel chair. "Miss Myrtle!" he exclaimed. He stood awkwardly, and the look on his face made it appear he'd just been asked to recite Hamlet's soliloquy when he hadn't memorized it.

The *Bradley Bugle's* office was a defiant relic of a bygone era. The place had a pungent aroma. A cocktail of ink, paper, and what could only be described as "essence of forgotten sandwich."

"Sloan," said Myrtle briskly. "There's been a change of plan."

Sloan looked confused. Myrtle wondered if he'd perhaps been dozing in his swivel chair before she'd walked in. He didn't seem to follow her train of thought. "Change of plan? You mean for the helpful hints column? If you're ready to run it, I can still get it into tomorrow's paper."

"No, no not the column. Remember the story on Teddy Hartfield?"

Sloan's frown deepened. "Oh, yeah. You were going to do a profile on him for Valentine's Day. Whatever happened to that piece?" He hastily added, "I mean, not that it's any trouble, of course." He was likely thinking he'd forgotten his homework in Myrtle's class enough that he could afford to be expansive when Myrtle forgot to turn in an article.

"Well, I decided to turn it into a different type of story. More of a human-interest story of a florist on his busiest day of the year. But now the article is undergoing a third iteration."

Sloan said slowly, "What's that?" He was looking uncomfortable, as if he knew what Myrtle was about to say.

"Teddy Hartfield was murdered. Miles and I found him just a little while ago."

Sloan looked over at Miles with pleading eyes, as if hoping Myrtle wasn't telling the truth. Miles gave him a solemn nod of confirmation in return.

Sloan sank back down in his chair, which squealed from the sudden weight. "Oh no. That's terrible news."

"Did you know Teddy?" asked Miles.

"Nope. But I know this means Miss Myrtle wants to run a crime story." Perspiration started dotting Sloan's large forehead. He turned on a nearby oscillating fan, despite the coolness of the February day.

"Of course I want to run a crime story," said Myrtle acerbically. "A crime has occurred. Our readers deserve to know what's happened. Perhaps they're also interested in why there seem to be constant attacks on local florists."

Sloan shook his head. "I wouldn't bring up that angle. You know how upset Red gets. He's trying to provide law and order to the citizens of Bradley, and he's doing a pretty good job. Making it seem like there's a serial killer targeting florists won't make him happy."

"Fine. There's no connection between those two cases anyway, since Lillian Johnson's murderer is behind bars. But I thought it might make a catchy headline." Myrtle was pleased Sloan appeared to accept that she was writing the story. They usually went through a ridiculous and time-consuming process where he argued Red didn't want her reporting on local crime.

Then Myrtle had to remind him she did a marvelous job, and that she was the best one to report on the crime since she'd been at the scene.

"So I'll get the story to you shortly, Sloan. That way you can juggle things around so it can be on the front page."

Sloan nodded morosely. "Okay." He paused. "You know Red doesn't want you reporting on this stuff, right?"

"I'm aware, yes. Now that you've duly warned me, I'll head back home so I can get cracking on the article." Myrtle strode to the door.

Sloan said, "Oh, one second. I did want to tell you something, Miss Myrtle. I know you've been aggravated for a while about the copyediting in the newspaper."

"There's copyediting going on? That's a surprise."

Sloan continued, "I thought it would find somebody to take care of the problem for me."

"Are you certain it's someone qualified? Someone who is actually acquainted with the King's English?"

Sloan seemed baffled by the sudden reference to the monarchy. "Um, yeah. I mean, yes. It's someone who understands English. You'll remember her. Imogen Winthrop."

Myrtle made a face as if she'd suddenly tasted a piece of very sour candy.

"Remember?" persisted Sloan. "She taught with you. High school English."

"Yes, yes, I remember Imogen Winthrop. For heaven's sake, I have full access to my cognitive abilities. I was simply surprised, that's all."

Sloan looked worried now. "You don't think she's a good pick?"

Myrtle didn't, but not for reasons related to Imogen's copy-editing skills. It had more to do with the fact she simply didn't like the prissy woman. When Myrtle retired, it had been with a sigh of relief that she wouldn't have to endure Imogen Winthrop any longer. And here it sounded as if she'd be a colleague of hers. She pressed her lips together in irritation.

"No, I suppose she's all right," said Myrtle. It was hardly a ringing endorsement. "The only problem with Imogen is that she's a complete Luddite."

Sloan wasn't sure what to make of that term, either. "Luddite, Miss M?"

"Yes, Sloan. A technophobe, in today's parlance. Meaning, Imogen doesn't use computers."

Sloan gave a relieved laugh. Perhaps he'd imagined that being a Luddite was some sort of heinous medical issue. Maybe a contagious one. "Oh, I see. No, we already talked about that. I'm making space for Miz Winthrop in the newsroom. She won't have to have anything emailed over to her."

"Wonderful," muttered Myrtle.

Chapter Four

They climbed into Miles's car. "Back to your house, then?"

"Yes. I do need to get the story written, especially with Sloan running it on the front page tomorrow."

Miles said, "Isn't it a good thing Sloan has hired someone to handle the copyediting? You've complained about the issues in the paper for as long as I've known you. It's obviously been a thorn in your side."

Myrtle said, "The problem is that *Imogen* is a thorn in my side. I taught with her for a million years, and she had a talent for turning even the smallest thing into a nightmare. We had weekly staff meetings, and Imogen would ask questions about the plainest details. The meetings would go on for hours. Everyone wanted to kill her."

"And yet she continued teaching, unscathed."

Myrtle said, "Yes. Although no one could stand her. She liked to hear herself talk. It was most annoying."

"You won't have to have staff meetings with Imogen at the newspaper," pointed out Miles helpfully.

"No, but it won't make a difference. Seeing her name on the newspaper's masthead will completely undo me every morning."

Miles said, "You were already completely undone by the daily grammatical blunders. Perhaps this will end up being better."

"It won't be better unless *I'm* the one copyediting the newspaper."

"I don't understand why Sloan didn't make you copyeditor in the first place," said Miles slowly.

"I've been ruminating on it, and I believe I know why. He said it was because I was already too busy with the crime reporting. But I'm convinced it's because I make him nervous."

Miles said, "You've always seemed to enjoy making him nervous."

"Yes, but it appears to be backfiring now." Myrtle sighed. "Everything has to be complicated. Sloan wouldn't listen to me when I tried dissuading him from using Imogen. I warned him she was a technophobe, and he said she was going to work in the newsroom with him. What I should have pointed out is, if there's a late-breaking story, Imogen will have to travel to the newsroom to copyedit. That means *Sloan* will have to travel to the newsroom to unlock it and show her the article. It'll be horribly inconvenient."

"It sounds as if Sloan has already made a decision."

"Yes, it does seem that way," said Myrtle reluctantly. "Perhaps I should focus my efforts in the other direction."

"With Imogen."

"That's right. I'll try to scare her off one way or another."

Miles paused. "You could cook for her. Tell her, now that you're colleagues again, you'll bring over special treats for her every day."

"How on earth will *that* help scare off Imogen?" asked Myrtle in exasperation.

Miles seemed to be trying to contain some sort of inconvenient emotion. "Well, the food would have to be awful, you see."

"I don't think I'd be able to *make* awful food. It would be too much of a stretch. And a waste of time, money, and food, besides. No, it'll have to be something else." She paused. "Unless I brought her a loaf of Elaine's bread, of course, claiming it was mine. That would do it."

"Poor Elaine," said Miles.

"Yes. I do love Elaine as if she were my own child. I only wish she'd stop inflicting her horrid hobbies on us."

Miles was silent, seeming deep in thought as they continued on their way to Myrtle's house. Myrtle frowned. "What's wrong, Miles? You're not lovelorn over some woman, are you? Since it's Valentine's Day, maybe you should just send her a card."

"I'm *not* lovelorn." He seemed to be thinking of a good excuse for his mood. "I haven't slept well the past couple of nights. That's likely the problem."

"You don't want to fall asleep now, though. Then you'll really be all messed up. You'll be up in the middle of the night."

Miles gave her a wry look. "That's hardly unusual."

Myrtle and Miles were fellow insomniacs. Ordinarily, Myrtle would wander over to Miles's house at two in the morning to work puzzles, watch boring animal documentaries, and drink coffee.

He pulled into her driveway and didn't appear to be getting out of the car. Myrtle's frown deepened. "You're not coming in?"

"You're writing an article, after all."

Myrtle said, "I think I can spare thirty minutes to watch the rest of our soap opera. We stopped on quite a cliffhanger. Geraldine just woke up from her twenty-year coma. And the entire town is trapped in a parallel universe. I can't wait to see what they do with those storylines."

"Just the same, I think I'll head back home."

"I'll check on you later," said Myrtle, feeling a surge of responsibility. Miles was decidedly off, that was for sure. Considering the amount of hand sanitizer he was constantly slathering on, a virus seemed unlikely. Still, Myrtle decided she should follow up, just in case.

Miles said, "I'll be fine. I'm just going to put my feet up. I may turn my phone off."

It was all most aggravating, having Miles out of sorts. Myrtle climbed out of the car and headed inside the house. He waved to her before heading back to his own place, a couple of doors down. "Peculiar," said Myrtle.

She opened her front door to see more aggravating and peculiar things. Puddin, allergic to cleaning as usual, was asleep on Myrtle's sofa, snoring enthusiastically in front of her game show. An overly caffeinated host was exclaiming, "Behind door number three is . . . a brand-new car!"

"Mindless drivel," muttered Myrtle, walking over to turn it off. She studied the living room. Some baseboards appeared to be cleaned rather haphazardly. Some of them didn't seem to be cleaned at all.

Puddin was clutching a bag of potato chips like a pillow in her arms.

"Puddin!" said Myrtle sharply.

She thought Puddin would start awake, looking guilty. Instead, she yawned and stretched, dumping the potato chips on the floor and scattering little bits everywhere.

"Puddin!" said Myrtle in a louder, angrier, and more commanding voice.

Puddin opened sullen eyes. "Needed to rest my back."

"You haven't done enough baseboard cleaning for your back to be complaining about anything. Plus, you've been eating my potato chips."

"Exercise makes me hungry," muttered Puddin.

"I've had enough of your nonsense today."

"I can go home?" Puddin's face lit up.

"No, you can finish the job I'm paying you to do. Then you can go home. I have something important to work on."

This whetted Puddin's curiosity. She stood, stretched again, then picked up the rag she'd been using to swipe ineffectually at the baseboards. "What're you workin' on?"

"A story for the newspaper."

Puddin looked scornful now. "One of them hints columns."

"Not this time. There was an incident while I was out today." Myrtle hesitated. On the one hand, she hated to feed Puddin's incessant appetite for gossip. On the other hand, she often knew helpful tidbits about the good citizens of Bradley, usually from her cousin Bitsy. The much-better housekeeper. Myrtle decided to throw a bit of information Puddin's way. "It so happens that Teddy Hartfield died today."

Puddin's eyes were like saucers. "The flower guy?"

"Yes, the florist."

"Heart attack? Stroke? Cancer?" asked Puddin.

"None of the above. It appears he was murdered."

Puddin gave a low whistle. "Is that so? Well, that's cars, ain't it?'

"Cars? What sort of foolishness are you muttering about now?"

"Cars! You know. When you're a bad person and then bad things happen to you."

Myrtle said, "I believe you mean karma."

"Whatever," said Puddin, looking sullen.

"Which implies that you don't think Teddy Hartfield was all that great of a guy."

Puddin shrugged. "I hear things." She cut her eyes across to Myrtle as if wanting her to ask more. Puddin liked to be the one knowing things.

Myrtle sighed. She supposed she'd have to play along if she wanted any additional information. "What kinds of things have you heard?"

"He was dating that woman. Linda."

Myrtle made a face. "Can you be more specific? There must be twenty or more Lindas in this town."

"Linda Lambert. Bitsy cleans for her."

Naturally she would. It irritated Myrtle once again that she could only afford the subpar housekeeper in the family. "Linda had reason to kill Teddy?"

"He dumped her," said Puddin with satisfaction.

"Well, I'm sure that was very annoying, but I'm not sure it would rise to the level of motive. Unless this Linda Lambert is a particularly sensitive soul. Anything else?"

"Nope," said Puddin, her font of information drying up. She yawned a tremendous yawn.

"It looks as if you should finish the baseboards, then go home and rest." Myrtle looked at her through narrowed eyes.

Puddin made a face at the baseboards, which remained impassively dirty. "Yeah."

"Why are you so sleepy? You're ordinarily at least alert when you're over here. But today, your eyelids are dropping."

Puddin raised a hand to her offending eyelids. "Dusty," she spat out. Dusty was Puddin's husband and Myrtle's yardman. "He's snoring. I can't stand it."

"Sleep in another room."

"Don't wanna sleep on the sofa," grumbled Puddin.

"Make *Dusty* sleep on the sofa."

"Won't." Puddin looked very indignant at this.

Myrtle disappeared down the hall and into her bedroom. She returned with a plastic baggie full of earplugs. "Here. You can't be falling asleep at work. That's outside the norm, even for you."

Puddin grumbled at the earplugs, but took them with alacrity.

"How were you cleaning the baseboards before?" asked Myrtle.

"Kneelin' and scrubbin.'"

Myrtle said, "Try to work smarter, not harder."

"Speak English," said Puddin. Her pale face was getting a surly expression on it now.

"I mean, use the mop to slide across the baseboards. Rinse the mop often. That will keep you from stooping, save your back, and possibly make my baseboards look better than the slapdash cleaning they were getting before."

Puddin gazed thoughtfully at the baseboards. "Okay."

And, thankfully, Puddin was soon finished with her chore and out of the house so Myrtle could write her article. But first, she decided to call Miles and check in on him. Miles was often something of an Eeyore, but she hadn't seen him quite so out of sorts. He didn't answer the phone. Sighing, she went to her computer and started typing the piece for Sloan.

Chapter Five

Myrtle was proofreading her story on Teddy Hartfield's murder when there was a tap at the door. Her daughter-in-law, Elaine, and her brilliant grandson, Jack, were standing outside.

"Happy Valentine's Day!" said Elaine. Jack grinned at his grandmother and handed her a large Valentine made of construction paper. It appeared to be covered with lots of white glue, glitter, stickers of various sorts (some of them stickers of dump trucks and planes), and a handprint. It was the best Valentine Myrtle had ever received.

"Look at this!" she said, pointing out the different amazing features of the card. "Look how beautiful it is. Thank you, Jack. Let's go inside and put it on the fridge."

Elaine was carrying a bag, and Myrtle feared its contents. Her fears were confirmed when Elaine said, "I brought you over some bread, Myrtle."

Myrtle controlled a visceral wince and said brightly, "How sweet of you, Elaine. I'll put the bag in the kitchen." Without even looking at the bread, Myrtle could tell it must be very dense indeed. The bag was heavy. Elaine must have realized this because she said, "I'll put it on the counter for you."

Elaine held up another bag. "I have something else for you."

Myrtle was proud that she didn't flinch. She was starting to feel she was being punished for something. "Do you?"

"Yes. I've found myself suddenly overwhelmed by bread starters. I thought maybe you'd like to try making bread." Elaine gave her a smile. "So I've put some in here for you to try." She quickly added, "But be sure not to bring any over to our house. We've already got more bread than we can handle."

"Why thank you, Elaine," said Myrtle. "That's very thoughtful of you. And with me making bread, you won't have to continue donating your lovely loaves to me."

"True," said Elaine, frowning. She was likely mentally trying to conjure future victims to foist bread on.

Jack went into Myrtle's coat closet and pulled out the basket of toys she kept for him there. He was happily playing with an interesting combination of blocks and trucks. Elaine sat on the sofa. "How has your Valentine's Day been?"

"You've obviously not been in touch with your husband today."

"With Red?" asked Elaine. "No, he hasn't checked in. Why? What's happened?"

Myrtle said, "Teddy Hartfield, the florist, has been murdered. Miles and I discovered him."

"What? How awful." She put her hand over her mouth. "Oh my gosh, Linda Lambert must be devastated."

Myrtle remembered Puddin mentioned Linda and Teddy had been dating. Actually, Puddin had mentioned Teddy dumped Linda. "You know Linda?"

"Not super well. But she's been part of my morning coffee group from time to time. I know she and Teddy were dating."

Myrtle said, "Puddin told me Teddy had recently dumped her."

Elaine's eyes grew wide. "Really? I haven't spoken to her lately. Wow. She must have been really upset about that. From what I could tell, she'd fallen totally in love with Teddy. Linda was always saying how beautiful his arrangements were and how driven Teddy was. She sounded completely taken in." Elaine put her hand over her mouth again. "Uh-oh. I guess that might make Linda a suspect, too. Red's sure to find out Teddy and Linda were dating."

"Did Linda ever talk about anybody Teddy might be having issues with? Somebody who wished him harm?"

Elaine shook her head wryly. "Not at our coffee group. Everybody always seems really perky there and likes pretending their lives are perfect. It's not the kind of thing where you air all your problems because they'd be gossiped about as soon as we left the coffeehouse."

"I did have a question for you, Elaine. When I was at Blossom Serenade, I happened to notice a loaf of your bread there. Did you, by chance, visit the florist?"

Elaine said wryly, "Fortunately, it was Red."

Myrtle raised her eyebrows. "You're saying that my son both remembered it was Valentine's Day *and* bought you flowers? I would have said he didn't have a romantic bone in his body." It also, most interestingly, put Red at the crime scene.

"Oh, he can be quite the romantic when he wants to be. Now, I'm not saying he got the correct date for Valentine's Day. He actually visited Blossom Serenade yesterday. He brought the flowers home on the 13th."

Myrtle smiled. "And he thinks *my* memory is deteriorating. I'm just impressed he was that close to the correct date. I bet he was pleased as punch with himself for remembering."

"Yes, he was bursting with pride. And, of course, I made a big fuss over both the flowers and Red."

Myrtle said, "It still doesn't explain what a loaf of your bread was doing there." But she felt it probably did. Red, desperately wanting to disperse the bread, had taken one of the inedible loaves to Teddy when he visited the florist. Myrtle's experience with Elaine's bread had been that its surface was a landscape of craggy peaks and valleys resembling a moonscape. Slicing into it would require more than a simple butter knife . . . perhaps power tools would be needed. In fact, it was the kind of substance that easily might survive a nuclear apocalypse.

Elaine said, in confirmation, "Oh, Red said he thought it would be nice to share some bread with Teddy. He told me he'd given him a loaf."

"And at least it was on the day prior to the murder. That certainly helps. It means Red isn't a suspect."

Myrtle's phone rang, and she glared at it. "I've got to leave, anyway," said Elaine. "Jack and I need to run by the store and pick up a few things. See you later."

Myrtle answered the phone as Elaine put away toys and collected Jack. It was Dana, Miles's daughter.

"Hey there, Myrtle. How are you doing?"

Myrtle said, "Everything is good. Happy Valentine's Day."

"The same to you! Listen, I'm sorry to bother you. I wanted to see if you'd talked to my dad today. I've tried calling him a few times, and I haven't been able to get through to him."

"Your dad probably has his phone turned off," said Myrtle. "He mentioned he might power the phone down. But yes, I spent time with him this morning. He seemed very tired and talked about getting some more sleep."

Dana sounded relieved. "Okay, that's good to hear. So he's feeling all right?"

Myrtle reflected on Miles's crabby mood. "He wasn't in a great mood, but he seemed to feel fine, aside from the tiredness. We did have something of a disturbing morning, however, which might have affected his mood. Your dad and I found someone he knows from chess club dead."

Dana was quiet on the other end. Then she said, "Oh, no. Poor Dad."

Myrtle said, "Yes, I felt bad for him." She paused. "I can run over there, if you'd like. Let him know that he needs to call you later."

Dana hesitated. "I hate to ask you to do that. The thing is, I don't believe he checks his voicemail messages."

"He'd hate to miss a call from you. I'll just run over there. Talk to you later, Dana."

When Myrtle opened her front door, Pasha, her feral black cat, stood outside, a wise look on her face.

"You want to walk to Miles's place with me, don't you? What a smart girl! Let's head over there and wake him up."

A cold February breeze suddenly started gusting, and Myrtle leaned heavily on her cane. Pasha walked close by her, looking from side to side as if searching for small rodents that she could quickly subdue and present to Myrtle for a Valentine's gift. Fortunately, all of them had scampered away, either sensing Pasha's presence or hearing the pronounced thump of Myrtle's cane on the sidewalk.

Myrtle rapped on Miles's door. Pasha watched her curiously. "He might be asleep," explained Myrtle. She peered through the window beside the door and was surprised to see that Miles wasn't asleep at all, but was looking at what appeared to be old photo albums. He hastily put them aside and hurried to the door when he spotted Myrtle there.

"I was just about to take a nap," he said, just a touch defensively.

Myrtle frowned, looking over at his chair across the room. "All right," she said slowly. "I just wanted to let you know that you might want to turn on your phone. Or unmute it. Dana was trying to reach you."

His eyes widened at the mention of his daughter. "Is everything okay?"

"Yes, everything is fine. She just wanted to say hi and was worried when she couldn't get in touch with you. I said I'd run over and tell you to call her when you had the chance. And now, I should finish proofreading that story for Sloan." She turned to head out the door, but then looked around again. "Would you like to go see Zoey Hartfield with me tomorrow?"

"Teddy's sister?"

Myrtle nodded. "I thought I'd express my sympathies. And bring her a casserole, of course."

Miles recoiled, and Myrtle frowned again. "I thought, since you were one of Teddy's friends, you might want to come."

Miles considered this, perhaps weighing his obligation to pay his respects with his concern over the casserole. He finally said, "Okay, that sounds good. What time?"

"Mid-morning? I'd say earlier, but I hate to show up too early at a grieving family member's household."

Miles's eyebrow raised at this, possibly because Myrtle hadn't shown such a compunction for past visits. "Good idea," he said. "See you then."

Chapter Six

The next morning dawned bright and sunny. Myrtle, however, was up far before the dawn, as usual. Her sweet Pasha had seen lights on in the house around four-thirty and had pawed gently at Myrtle's front door. Pasha, although feral, knew she was always welcome. The cat rarely wanted to be inside the house, but when temperatures dipped precipitously, as they did in the early-morning hours of February fifteenth, she decided it was a fine place to warm herself.

Pasha was also very preoccupied with Myrtle's peculiar movements in the kitchen. Myrtle was working from an old recipe card in an equally old recipe book that had belonged to her mother. The card for paprika chicken casserole had various foreign splashes and smudges on it from years ago. But Myrtle was always happy when she pulled it out and saw her mother's handwriting.

Myrtle had been certain she'd had all the ingredients for the dish before she started. However, looking at the card, she realized some substitutions would need to be in order. She had no yellow pepper, for one thing, but felt zucchini might be acceptable in its place. There was no cornstarch in Myrtle's pantry, but she was certain using the same amount of flour would work just fine. Slightly more concerning was the absence of paprika, for which the casserole was named. However, she was confident that cayenne pepper would work perfectly, considering it was the same color.

Further along into the cooking process, Myrtle saw that a can of tomatoes was required. She had no desire to traipse to the Piggly Wiggly grocery store, even if it had been open at such an early hour. It was then she made the executive decision to substitute ketchup, which was basically the same thing. After compiling the casserole, she shoved it into the oven and started working on the daily crossword.

Miles arrived shortly before nine-thirty. As usual, he was neatly dressed in khakis and a button-down shirt. His eyes were tired, though.

Myrtle studied him closely. "Did you sleep last night?"

"Not particularly, but that's hardly newsworthy. Neither of us sleeps well on a regular basis."

This was true. However, when Miles needed to catch up on sleep, he ordinarily was able to do it. Myrtle let it pass. "Did you have a nice conversation with Dana? You did remember to call her, didn't you?"

"I did. And it was a great chat." Miles stopped still, sniffing the air suspiciously. "What's that I smell?"

"Paprika chicken casserole."

Miles frowned. "It smells rather spicy."

"Well, paprika is spicy. At least, it's a spice."

Miles tilted his head to one side, still sniffing. "It really doesn't smell like paprika to me."

"Oh, that's right. I had to substitute cayenne pepper, instead. I was out of paprika."

Miles looked panicky. "Myrtle, you can't do that."

"Do what?"

Miles said, "You can't hand someone a casserole and misrepresent what it is. That's false advertising. And poor Zoey Hartfield is a grieving sister."

"It's absolutely fine, Miles. It's always the thought that counts. Besides, the only thing that's different is the spice used. It's not like I'm calling it chicken and putting venison in there." She managed to forget or disregard the zucchini and ketchup substitutions. "Now let's head on over there before Zoey goes to run errands or something."

Miles was again rather quiet in the car, which Myrtle attributed to sleepiness. "I do require my sidekick to be awake for the investigation. You know I depend on you."

"Do you? I'm not sure I'm all that useful in these suspect interviews, Myrtle. I'm mostly just a figure in the background."

Myrtle said, "Yes, but you keep me on my toes. And you look respectable. If I start asking sensitive questions, you lull the suspects into thinking I'm simply being a gossipy, nosy, old lady."

"Glad I can be of assistance," said Miles dryly. "And where exactly are we headed? I'm just driving aimlessly right now."

"You're driving in the right direction. But you'll need to take a right at Sage Street."

Myrtle continued directing him until they reached a small home with weathered siding. It must have once been a rather vibrant blue, but now resembled more of a washed-out sky. The lawn was overgrown and sported dandelions and clover. The mailbox leaned precariously, its rusty door hanging on for dear life.

Miles frowned. "Are you sure this house is occupied? Maybe Zoey moved somewhere else."

"I'm afraid this is it. I think Zoey might need some help."

Miles's frown deepened. "You *do* know Zoey, don't you? We're not just showing up with a counterfeit paprika chicken casserole at a stranger's home?"

"Of course not! Zoey was a former student of mine. And you must know her, since you knew her brother."

Miles said, "She never showed up at chess tournaments." He paused as he parked on the broken cement of the driveway. "What sort of a student was she?" He said this as if suspecting she must not have been at the top of her class.

"Wretched. Zoey never handed in her homework. And never even *did* it. I remember she summarized *The Catcher in the Rye* by saying it was about a baseball player. At that moment, I'd considered early retirement and wept for the future of our country."

Miles said, "But you kept on teaching."

"Money, Miles. Maintaining an income is a great motivator. Plus, I did enjoy many of the kids. Most of the days were fun, aside from some moments of general foolishness and nonsense."

They carefully picked their way down an overgrown walkway to Zoey's front door. Myrtle rang the bell, which she couldn't hear ringing. She decided to hedge her bets and knock loudly.

"Coming! Coming!" said a voice from inside. When the door opened, it revealed a woman in her early fifties with silver streaks in her brown hair. Worry lines etched her face, and she wore an outfit of mismatched garments. Her gray eyes looked exhausted.

"Miss Myrtle," she said in surprise. "It's nice to see you." Her features brightened.

"So good to see you, Zoey. This is my friend, Miles Bradford."

Miles put out his hand, and Zoey shook it in a loose handshake.

"I've brought you a favorite casserole of mine," said Myrtle, presenting it. "Paprika chicken."

Miles muttered something indistinguishable, and Myrtle shot him a look.

"Gracious, that's so nice of you." Zoey looked behind her into the dim interior of her house as if weighing whether she should invite her guests in. Myrtle affected to look as frail as possible, which was very difficult for a big-boned woman of her height. "Please come in," said Zoey quickly, likely concerned Myrtle might have a fainting spell on her front porch.

Myrtle felt as if she might need a flashlight to navigate her way to a chair. Going from the sunny February outdoors to the darkness inside was quite a change. As her eyes adjusted, she saw there were heavy curtains drawn all the way closed.

Zoey seemed to realize her guests' vision might be impaired. "Sorry," she said quickly, moving across the small room to pull the curtains open. Once she did, a threadbare floral sofa, piles of dusty novels, and an antique radio were revealed.

Myrtle and Miles perched on the sofa. Miles was twitchy, likely longing to pull out his hand sanitizer, which was his usual go-to when he felt he was in a place that needed tidying. Puddin would have despaired at the work that needed to be done in Zoey's house. It was blanketed with dust and clearly hadn't seen a vacuum in quite some time. Aside from that, it wasn't messy or cluttered. It just wasn't clean.

Zoey said with a faded smile, "I'll just put this casserole away. Lovely of you to bring it."

As she rushed off, Myrtle and Miles exchanged a look. Zoey's fortunes were clearly not as good as her brother's. Could money possibly be a motive for her to murder Teddy? Myrtle wondered what Teddy's will might reveal.

Zoey returned to them, sitting in a precariously wobbly armchair next to the sofa. "Thanks so much for this," she said.

Myrtle said, "We were just so sorry about Teddy. Miles here played chess with your brother. Such a terrible shock."

With that, any emotional defenses Zoey had erected collapsed immediately. Myrtle and Miles looked on in horror as Zoey started wailing.

"Tissues, tissues," muttered Myrtle desperately, fumbling through her massive purse for a packet. Finally finding it, she thrust the entire thing at Zoey. "There, there," said Myrtle ineffectively.

It took a few minutes for Zoey to settle down. Myrtle supposed she should be accustomed to grief at her age. Somehow, she always found it very troubling, mostly because she had no idea what to do. Miles clearly felt equally at a loss, until he brightened, remembering a glass of water might help. Or at least get him out of the room. Myrtle continued with her there-theres until Miles returned with water and Zoey's sobbing lessened.

The water arrived just in time since Zoey had now commenced hiccupping. She took a large gulp, then another. A minute later, the storm was over.

Zoey gave them an apologetic look. "I'm so sorry. I hadn't cried at all since I heard the news."

"I'm sorry to have triggered it," said Myrtle. Sorry and rather horrified, that was.

Zoey shook her head. "No, no, I needed to let it all out. I feel much better now. Yesterday, the news was such a shock that I felt numb all day long." She wiped her eyes with a tissue, looking at Myrtle. "Red came over to talk with me a couple of times."

Myrtle gave her a grim smile. "I do hope he was sensitive."

"Well, he certainly was when he was informing me about Teddy's death. I have the feeling that's a duty he's had to endure quite a few times during the course of his job. But then he apologized and told me he had to ask the same questions he asked everyone else who knew Teddy. Meaning Red thinks I'm a suspect." Zoey swallowed hard. "And I didn't have an alibi. None. I'm sure I'm a *prime* suspect, now."

Myrtle clucked. "I'm sure you're not. Red just has to follow protocol, dear. You know how it is. I'm certain *many* people don't have alibis."

"I'm not positive about that. I wish I'd stuck to my original plan for the day. I'd gotten up early yesterday to look at job postings and drop off my resume. But when I checked online, there wasn't anything new listed. The only things available were stuff I wasn't qualified to do or manual labor, which I'm getting a little long-in-the-tooth for. So instead of going out and asking to apply for jobs, I binge-watched a TV show I'd been wanting to see."

"What was it?" asked Miles, curiously. He'd told Myrtle days ago that he was looking for something new to watch. Myrtle wasn't any help since she really only watched one TV show regularly—her soap opera.

"Oh, it was a British crime drama. Let's see, what was the name of it? *East End Enigma.* That was it. Very entertaining, if a little gory from time to time. But you can always look away."

Myrtle could tell Miles was no longer interested in the crime drama. He was far too squeamish for television that he had to turn away from.

"Anyway, I was curled up on the sofa with a blanket and some popcorn, and turned my phone off. I didn't know anything about Teddy until Red knocked on my door to let me know." Tears sprang to her eyes again, but she rapidly blinked them away.

Myrtle said, "Terrible, terrible news. Were you and Teddy very close?"

"We got along well. We were the only family we had, you know. You might remember, Miss Myrtle, our dad left when we were little. Our mom died just a few years ago. So Teddy and I always celebrated holidays together and that sort of thing." Zoey paused. "We shared a strong bond. Teddy would confide in me and vice-versa. We both wanted to travel the world, try new things." Her voice broke on the last few words. She continued after a moment. "I can't believe he'll never be able to do the things he wanted."

Miles cleared his throat. "Teddy mentioned you a few times when we were at chess club. He seemed very fond of you."

A flicker of surprise crossed Zoey's features before it was quickly hidden. "Thank you for letting me know. In some ways, even though Teddy was younger, he was sort of like a big brother to me. He was always so responsible. He helped me fix a leaky roof or a running toilet. He'd stop by with treats from the grocery store after he'd done his own shopping." She shrugged. "Just a great guy. And this is a total waste."

Myrtle nodded sympathetically. "It certainly is, dear. I'm sorry it's been such a long while since I've seen you. How have you been doing?" She carefully didn't let her gaze wander over the faded furnishings of the living room.

Zoey made a face. "Not very well. But you might not be surprised by that, Miss Myrtle. I wasn't exactly a superstar student when I was in your class. I don't know why I thought I'd be able to get some amazing, well-paying job. But you know how it is when you're a kid—you think you can be an astronaut. Nobody ever tells you exactly how much math you have to take to be an astronaut."

Myrtle raised an eyebrow. "Is that what you wanted to be? An astronaut?"

"No, I actually wanted to be a brain surgeon."

Miles said, "Which also involves taking math. And lots of science."

"Exactly. But you know how it is. Your mom isn't going to tell you you'll never make it into med school. She's going to tell you that you can be anything you want to be."

Myrtle asked, "What did you end up being?"

"A customer service representative. Nobody dreams of being one of those." Zoey sighed and rubbed her eyes, which only succeeded in making them look redder. "I haven't always made the smartest decisions in my life, either. I'm pretty much financially illiterate. I'm drowning in credit card debt, my rent is in arrears. And now, I've been fired from my job, which is why I was planning on job hunting yesterday morning."

"Heavens," said Myrtle. "That's a run of horrible luck."

"Yes. Even worse, the company said they won't give me a good reference, even though I've worked for them for the past three years. How am I supposed to find a job with a three-year gap on my resume?"

Myrtle asked delicately, "And your husband?"

Zoey snorted. "We're divorced. I took my name back. And that divorce cost me tons of money. I was so desperate to get rid of the guy that money didn't seem important to me. But boy, I'm feeling it now." She shook her head. "I can't catch a break. Teddy and I had this spinster aunt who died a couple of years ago. We understood forever that Teddy and I were going to be her heirs and split her estate. But then she decided I wasn't responsible enough to get an inheritance. She said I 'wasn't financially responsible.'"

"Did she have reason to believe that?" asked Myrtle delicately.

Zoey pressed her lips together. Then she said, "Like I said, I made some bad financial decisions. The credit card thing was one of them. I don't do a great job taking care of my things, either, so our aunt might have felt I don't care. I'm sure you saw the state of the yard and the house when you drove up. But she didn't understand how, when you're worried about money all the time, you don't have the energy to do anything else. All your energy is focused on getting your next paycheck."

"You must have been very disappointed when you were written out of your aunt's will."

Zoey snorted. "That's one way to put it. Mad would be another."

Miles cleared his throat. "So Teddy received the entire inheritance? Or did your aunt find a charity to bequeath part of her estate to?"

"Oh, Teddy got the whole thing. I was pretty mad about that. I thought about contesting the will, but lawyers cost money." She paused. "I guess Teddy might have left me money in his will, though."

"Did he have one?" asked Myrtle. Sometimes younger people felt they were invincible.

"I'm sure he did. Teddy was always a responsible guy."

Myrtle nodded. That seemed to go along with owning his own business. "Have you any ideas about who might have done this? Was there anyone who had a grudge against Teddy?"

"Absolutely," said Zoey. "Ollie Spearman."

Miles pushed his glasses up his nose. "I believe he worked with Teddy at the shop?"

"Ollie did work with him for a while. Until Teddy forced him out of Blossom Serenade."

Myrtle asked, "Why did he do that? Was Ollie irresponsible?"

"Not at all. At least, not a normal person's definition of irresponsible. But like I just said, Teddy was always super-responsible. Compared to Teddy, Ollie probably didn't seem like he was up to snuff."

Miles said, "And Teddy fired him."

"That's right. Although Teddy was trying to say Ollie quit the shop voluntarily. Ollie would never have left on his own. He loved that place. But Teddy didn't like Ollie's floral arrangements. He kept saying Ollie's designs didn't 'fit the aesthetic of Blossom Serenade.' I didn't even understand what he meant by that. And then there's the problem with Linda."

Myrtle sat up straighter. "Linda Lambert? She was dating Teddy, wasn't she? I understand they'd recently broken up." At least, that's what Puddin had said.

"That's right. Teddy had dumped her. Linda had dated Ollie before Teddy started seeing her, so there were bad feelings surrounding that."

Miles said slowly, "Surely the bad feelings would have been on Ollie's part and not Teddy's."

"Yep. Ollie wasn't happy that Teddy stole his girlfriend. So between getting fired and having Teddy take Linda away, Ollie had plenty of reasons to want Teddy dead."

Then Zoey changed the subject, bringing up her old school days and talking about the high school. They chatted for another ten minutes before Myrtle and Miles brought their visit to a close.

Chapter Seven

B ack in Miles's car, Myrtle said, "Well, that was interesting."
"Zoey's house was in pretty terrible shape," said Miles. "She really seems to be struggling financially."

"I know. I feel even better about bringing over the casserole."

Miles muttered, "Considering her circumstances, Zoey might actually eat it."

"What was that, Miles?"

"I said that Zoey will be excited to eat it."

Myrtle nodded. "I was thinking the same thing. Perhaps I should bring her another one later on."

Miles wisely didn't air his thoughts on this idea. "What did you make of her relationship with Teddy?"

"It sounded like it was a good one, didn't it? Teddy helped Zoey out with repairs and whatnot."

Miles said, "Except Zoey didn't seem pleased about losing her half of her inheritance."

Myrtle shrugged. "It was Zoey's own doing. It's one thing to be poor. I'm fairly poor. It's another thing to be fiscally irresponsible. It certainly wasn't Teddy's fault that their aunt decided Zoey was a terrible choice for a windfall. Naturally, Zoey was disappointed, but she has only herself to blame."

"Curtis was right that Ollie hadn't been at the shop for a couple of weeks. And now we know it wasn't because of a vacation."

Myrtle said, "Precisely. I wonder what Ollie's next move is."

"It was pretty awful of Teddy to fire him because he didn't like his floral arrangements. You'd think that would be something the two of them could have worked out."

Myrtle said, "It was worse of Teddy to steal Ollie's girlfriend."

Miles made a face. "Yes. That wasn't very honorable behavior."

Myrtle knew this was quite a condemnation for Miles. Miles had always been very particular about his honor. She said, "Well, Curtis said earlier that it was Teddy's way or the highway. I guess firing Ollie is an example of that."

"Still, you'd think that Teddy would have simply sat down with Ollie and told him he needed to change the style of his arrangements."

"Maybe he did. Or maybe he was simply sick of Ollie's arrangements not selling. Regardless, it was ultimately Teddy's business. He could run it as he saw fit," said Myrtle. She looked over at Miles. "Did you ever get an inkling of what Teddy was really like? It sounds like you might have been acquainted with a different version of him."

Miles shook his head. "Teddy seemed easy-going to me."

"Hmm. Was he winning, though? When he was playing you?"

"Always," said Miles without rancor.

"That might have been why he was so easy-going. I wonder if others of your chess friends had the same experience with Teddy."

"I suppose I could ask them," said Miles slowly.

"I'd be interested to hear what they say. I'm thinking that perhaps Teddy was a very competitive person. Maybe Ollie is actually very talented at arranging flowers. That could have been the real reason Teddy wanted to get rid of him. And I'm wondering what Ollie's doing now that he's lost his job and his girlfriend."

"Perhaps murdering former employers?" suggested Miles.

"It's certainly a possibility."

Miles pulled his car into Myrtle's driveway. "Coming inside?" she asked.

"I think I'll go home and relax for a little while," he said.

"Suit yourself," said Myrtle. "I'm going to eat breakfast."

"I thought you'd already eaten breakfast."

Myrtle said, "That was ages ago. It's time for a second breakfast." With that, Myrtle headed to her front door.

A few minutes later, she was eating a nice meal involving eggs, bacon, and cheese grits. Pasha peered in through the kitchen window as she was making it, and she'd let her in, giving her half a can of cat food. Now Pasha was languidly bathing herself at Myrtle's feet.

There was a knock on the front door. "I bet that's Miles," Myrtle told Pasha. "He'll want to watch the tape of *Tomorrow's Promise*. I knew he wanted to find out what happened with that parallel universe."

But when she opened the door, it was Wanda, her psychic friend, on the doorstep.

Myrtle beamed at her. "Wanda! What a wonderful surprise. Come in, come in."

Pasha was even more delighted to see Wanda. She wrapped herself around Wanda's legs until Wanda gingerly sat on the floor and devoted time to petting her. "Love you, Pasha," she said gruffly.

"How about a big plate of breakfast food?" asked Myrtle. "I've still got all the stuff out on the counter. Eggs, cheese grits, bacon?"

Wanda nodded shyly. "I kin do it, if you want."

"Pasha would never forgive me if I cut short your time with her. Let me just polish off this food of mine for just a second."

Soon Myrtle was putting a full plate of food in front of Wanda. Pasha sat in another chair at the kitchen table, watching Wanda with enormous eyes. When Myrtle wasn't looking, Wanda gave the cat a tiny bite of bacon, which Pasha devoured in a millisecond.

"How are you doing?" asked Myrtle.

"All right," said Wanda. She looked over at Myrtle's fridge. "Nice valentine."

"Isn't it beautiful? Jack made it himself." Myrtle suddenly frowned. "It just occurred to me that you must have spent Valentine's Day alone since your brother married and moved out."

Wanda nodded, looking completely unconcerned.

"But that's terrible! You should have come over."

Wanda drawled, "Thought yew might have plans."

"Me? Not on Valentine's Day. All I had was a delightful, albeit brief, visit with my grandson."

"An' a murder," said Wanda.

"Yes. And a murder. I do forget sometimes that you're a psychic." She tilted her head to one side, looking curiously at Wanda. "I have the feeling I know what you're going to say, but I still have to ask the question. Do you have any inklings about what happened to Teddy Hartfield?"

Wanda gave her a sorrowful look. "The Sight—"

"Yes, I know. The Sight doesn't work that way. It's a pity, isn't it? Think of all the knowledge and power you could harness."

Wanda ate another forkful of her scrambled eggs. "I do got one thang for yew."

"What's that? Wait, don't tell me. I'm in danger."

Wanda gave a small, sad smile. "Yep, yew are. But what I was gonna say is a change of habit is important." She paused. "That's all I got."

Myrtle repeated the statement under her breath. "But what does that mean? Do I need to change *my* habits? Does it mean I should turn in earlier, like Red is always saying? Or is someone else's change of habit significant?"

Wanda gave her a helpless shrug. "It's all I got."

Myrtle nodded. "Well, thanks. I'll keep that in mind."

Wanda polished off her bacon and took a spoonful of her cheese grits. "Also thinkin' about Miles."

"Are you?" asked Myrtle eagerly. "Because I haven't been able to figure out Miles the last couple of days. I'd love some sort of insight."

"He's got an aura."

Myrtle said, "A very cranky aura."

"A sad one. Very sad. About Valentine's Day."

Myrtle made a face. "Yet another reason to dislike the day. It's been manufactured by greeting card people, anyway. Why on earth is he sad about the holiday?"

Wanda helplessly shrugged again. "Jest is."

"Okay. I'll ask him about it later. You've got all sorts of information this morning, Wanda."

"Got some more, too. We should git to town hall."

Myrtle frowned. "Surely there's not some sort of ghastly emergency at town hall. The police department is right next door."

"Nope, jest a meetin'. That developer guy is there."

"Ah, I'm following you now," said Myrtle. "The one Curtis was talking about. Teddy foiled his attempts to develop his own property because Teddy was trying to protect an endangered species in the stream there."

Wanda nodded solemnly.

"Nat Drake, I believe his name is. Yes." Myrtle looked at Wanda in amazement. "That's yet another clairvoyant moment for you today."

"Nope. Heard it on the radio comin' over. Want me to drive us there?"

Wanda had a used car that was new to her. Actually, driving itself was new to Wanda. Miles and Myrtle had recently helped her find her vehicle, and she loved it. "Yes," said Myrtle. "Let's drive."

Wanda was such a careful driver that it took quite a bit of time to reach their destination. But finally, they reached town hall. Wanda drove around the back of the building to park there. Judging from the many available parking spaces, it appeared the town hall meeting wasn't heavily attended. But then, it was the middle of the day on a Thursday in February. The timing made Myrtle wonder if town hall was eager to pass something without any irritating constituents in attendance. Fortunately, she did know one town hall representative. Tippy Chambers was Myrtle's book club president, garden club president, and heavily involved in Myrtle's church. Usually, it was rather annoying that Tippy was so very hard to escape. Today, however, it was nice to be able to speak to her, which Myrtle fully intended to do following the meeting.

Unfortunately, they had one hurdle to jump before making their way to the meeting. Red was there. Myrtle surveyed her son with displeasure.

Red's eyebrows flew up. "Mama! What are you doing here?" He gave a courteous nod to Wanda, who gave him a gap-toothed grin in response.

"I'm being a responsible member of the community," said Myrtle with a sniff.

"That's unlikely."

Myrtle narrowed her eyes. "I'm attending the development hearing." Myrtle didn't, in fact, know whether it was a development meeting at all. But considering the fact that a developer was in attendance, she figured it was a good bet.

"Because you want to weigh in on new development?"

Myrtle sniffed. "Somebody should. Otherwise, these developers run rampant. They do whatever they want. Weighing in means that I'm a good citizen."

Red tilted his head to one side. "You're sure your presence here has nothing to do with the fact Nat Drake is here?"

"Who?" asked Myrtle innocently.

Wanda looked down at the floor with great interest.

Red abandoned that line of questioning. "You've never gone to these meetings before."

"Yes, well, it's part of my self-improvement program."

"There are other ways you could focus on self-improvement. What about a sittercise class? You could get healthier by simply sitting."

Myrtle glared at her son. "But it's *not* simply sitting. That's the whole point. It's exercising. You're sitting, but you're moving your arms and legs in various directions."

"Whatever. Or, here's a good idea. Why not work on your sleep hygiene? You don't do a good job with that."

Myrtle said, "I have no idea what you're talking about. Sleep hygiene? It sounds like something you've made up."

"Not a bit. I was reading about it online just the other day. You should be going to bed at the same time every night. You shouldn't be looking at screens for an hour before turning in. And you should make sure your bedroom is dark and cool. I can send you the article, if you'd like to read it."

Myrtle raised her chin. "No thank you. Now, if you'll let Wanda and me through, we're going to perform our civic duty."

Chapter Eight

The town hall meeting room was sparsely populated, making it easy for Wanda and Myrtle to sit near the front. The commissioners were already in their seats behind the long desk, facing the audience. Tippy blinked as she spotted Myrtle and Wanda, then gave them a wave, which they returned.

Wanda said, "That's him." She nodded her head toward a man in his late-thirties, who carried himself with a preppy elegance. His sandy-blond hair was meticulously styled, and his piercing blue eyes appeared to dissect the world around him. He was wearing a tailored navy blazer, a crisp white shirt, and designer loafers. To Myrtle, he looked like a very successful man.

Red sat in the front row, far to the left of his mother and Wanda. The meeting was called to order. This was followed by several minutes of very boring talk from several of the commissioners, who Myrtle believed likely loved hearing their own voices.

Finally, it was time to get down to business. Nat stated he had purchased a building in downtown Bradley and was planning to develop it into a mixed-use residential and commercial building, with residential on the top floor and businesses on the bottom. The commissioners asked a few questions about this. There was apparently a zoning change that was going to have to take place because the area wasn't currently zoned for any sort of residential use whatsoever. Tippy asked a question regarding the exterior design of the building, apparently wanting to ensure that it was going to match the rest of the properties downtown. Nat quickly reassured her that would be the case.

Myrtle, having gotten spotty sleep the night before, found herself starting to doze off. Wanda was already ahead of her, chin nearly touching her chest.

Tippy cleared her throat, looking directly at Myrtle and Wanda. "I see we have some members of the public in attendance today. Thanks for coming. I'd like to give you the opportunity to speak or ask questions."

Red turned to look at Myrtle, scowling. She pressed her lips together in annoyance. Red was sure to give her a hard time later if she didn't speak. But she really didn't have questions. Still, she stood and walked over to the rather unnecessary microphone that was stationed nearby. "Yes, I have a question. I'd like to know what commercial enterprises will be occupying the proposed development."

Red rolled his eyes.

Nat gave her a tight smile. "That's as yet undetermined. We'll start looking for tenants after everything is approved and our renovation is completed."

"Is there anything else?" asked Tippy.

Myrtle shook her head and took her seat. The commissioners took a vote, and the development was approved.

Nat was apparently not in the mood to hang around and schmooze with the commissioners. He gave them a quick thanks, then headed for the exit. Red gave his mother a hard stare as she and Wanda hurriedly followed suit. He looked as if he might be ready to give chase, but then he was stopped by an elderly commissioner who wanted to bend his ear for a few minutes.

Myrtle was able to catch up with Nat shortly before he climbed into the largest SUV she'd ever laid eyes on. "Mr. Drake," she called.

He stopped, turning around. Then he gave her a 100-watt smile. "Hi there. Thanks for your interest in the project today. Are you considering residing in the finished building?"

"Hmm? Oh. No, I'm just on my neighborhood watch. I give my neighbors updates on various things in town. They just love those kinds of details."

Nat looked amused. "Do they? That's great they're so interested. If you want to email them the pertinent information, I know the meetings are transcribed and released online."

Myrtle already knew this. But she also knew Nat Drake appeared to be the kind of man who enjoyed knowing things. And explaining what he knew. So she affected a grateful expression. "That's wonderful. What a great idea."

Nat regarded her thoughtfully. "I believe I know who you are. Myrtle Clover, aren't you?"

It pleased Myrtle to be recognized. "That's right. And I'm with my friend, Wanda."

Nat didn't give Wanda more than a passing glance. In Myrtle's mind, it was a strike against him. He continued, "You're Red's mother, aren't you?"

Ah. Myrtle suspected she knew now why Nat was interested in speaking with her. "Yes. You know Red?"

"Naturally. Although I'm afraid our relationship is somewhat strained right now. He was glowering at me during the meeting."

"Was he?" asked Myrtle. "How odd. Why would he do such a thing?" Myrtle was quite sure Red was glowering at *her* and not a bit at Nat. But then, she had no desire to disclose that, since she wanted to hear what was on Nat's mind.

"Yes. I believe he thinks I'm upset about a development project that had to be scrapped because of Teddy."

Myrtle smiled at him. "I'd think you were an unusually patient person if you *weren't* upset."

He gave her a wry smile. "You're right. I was upset. Still am upset, actually. But I certainly wouldn't have gained anything from murdering Teddy. It's not like I can move forward with the project now that Teddy's dead. The salamanders are still there. They're still endangered. It would have solved nothing."

Myrtle gave him a sweet smile. "I don't suppose you would do something like that for revenge? It seems many people murder for that reason. Hard to imagine, of course."

"No, I wouldn't. I don't want to go to jail. I have a booming business, I'm doing well, and I'd like to reap my rewards instead of whiling the hours away behind bars." He paused. "Perhaps you can tell Red that."

"Perhaps." Myrtle didn't mention the fact she was out of contact with Red whenever humanly possible. "Were you able to give Red an alibi? I'd think that would be a great way to keep him off your back."

"Unfortunately, honest people don't think about alibis too often. I was dealing with odds and ends at the house yesterday morning. Teddy Hartfield was the last person on my mind." Myrtle wasn't completely sure he was telling the truth, however. She wondered if Wanda felt the same. He was fidgeting quite a bit and not completely holding eye contact.

Myrtle decided not to call him on it, instead giving him a sympathetic look. "Housework is a never-ending chore, isn't it?"

"Yes. I was chasing down elusive socks, watering my houseplants, and texting my girlfriend. Aside from that, I was tying up loose ends on another project, via email. It was just an ordinary day."

"What did you make of Teddy?" asked Myrtle curiously.

Nat shrugged. "I didn't really know him. This was the first time I'd met him—over the salamander thing, I mean. I had no idea he was any sort of environmental activist. That caught me totally off-guard. I'd heard of Teddy, of course, but only that he was the guy to order flowers from if I wanted a special arrangement for my girlfriend."

Myrtle wanted to hear more about the salamander issue from Nat's point of view. She tilted her head to one side. "How exactly did the salamanders shut down the development project? I'm only slightly familiar with the story."

Nat was looking just a smidgeon impatient, as if he were ready to head off in his tremendous SUV to do Very Important

Work. But he was clearly also hoping Myrtle would talk with her police chief son on his behalf. He said, "Well, Teddy managed to get my planned development blocked because of the stream running through part of the property. That stream was the habitat of the Eastern Hellbender."

"Gracious! What a terrible name."

"It's a pretty terrible-looking animal," said Nat wryly. "Especially to the crayfish they eat. It's nobody's pretty child. Apparently, it's a giant salamander. The average length is nearly a foot and a half, I'm told."

"What I don't really understand is why Teddy took such an interest in this animal. How did he even know about the salamander in the stream? Did he visit your property and go looking for endangered species?"

Nat said, "The property I own abuts Teddy's property. So Teddy had a direct interest in preserving it." Before Myrtle could say anything, he added, "My intentions were to be very responsible with the development. It was meant to help revitalize the community with new commercial spaces, housing, and infrastructure that would attract businesses, create jobs, and boost the local community."

It sounded as if Nat was reciting from memory the speech he must have given in front of the town commissioners at the time. It sounded slightly unnatural, like a stump speech or a polished soundbite.

Nat continued, "There were going to be affordable housing units since I believe strongly that everyone deserves a safe and comfortable place to be, regardless of income. The commissioners were all very excited about the project."

"Gracious. How big is that property? And so near to downtown? It must be quite valuable."

"Acres of woodlands. I'd bought it years ago and waited to develop it. Part of the woodlands were going to be preserved as green spaces." He made a face. "Instead, it was all abandoned."

"No wonder you were upset," said Myrtle.

Nat gave her a sharp look. "Not upset enough to murder Teddy. It was annoying, but things like that happen in this business. Yes, it held potential financial gains for me. And I was irritated that I was holding a piece of property that could no longer feasibly be developed. But I wasn't going to kill anybody over it. It was just a professional disappointment."

"Is there anybody you can think of who might have something against Teddy?"

Nat nodded. "I've been thinking about that. Perhaps that's something you can tell Red, as well. Curtis Walsh. Do you know him?"

Myrtle nodded. "I spoke with him yesterday. He lives next door to Teddy, I believe."

"That's right." Nat sighed. "One thing Red has focused on is that my fingerprints were found at the shop."

"Probably half the town of Bradley's fingerprints are there."

"Exactly," said Nat eagerly. "That's what I was telling him. I did go by there in person one day to try to reason with Teddy. I wanted him to back off about the salamander."

"But weren't you saying that wouldn't do any good?"

Nat said, "This was before Teddy contacted the Environmental Protection Agency."

Myrtle raised her eyebrows. "I see. So the Hellbender Sala-mander is listed as endangered by the Federal Endangered Species Act."

"That's right. Like I was telling you, once Teddy spilled the beans to them, there was no way the development was going to move forward. If I *was* going to murder Teddy, it would have made a lot more sense for me to have done it weeks ago."

Myrtle nodded. Nat would then have been preventing the whistleblower, so to speak.

"Anyway, I went by to see if Teddy could be persuaded to drop the whole matter. He couldn't be, though." Nat shrugged. "So that was the end of that. But while I was there, Curtis Walsh came bursting into the shop, screaming about something that had happened that morning. Curtis had a climbing wall he'd built for his son. His son fell, breaking his arm. Curtis wasn't able to leave his driveway because he was blocked in by a deliv-ery truck."

"Mercy," said Myrtle. "Couldn't he drive off-road a little and get around it?"

"Apparently not. There's a ditch at the front of his yard. Cur-tis was steaming, he was so furious." Nat turned his arm to look at what appeared to be a Rolex watch. "Sorry, but I'm going to have to get going. I have a meeting I need to attend in a few min-utes." He looked again at Wanda and said slowly, "You seem very familiar."

Wanda blushed, shaking her head. "Don't know yew."

Myrtle, who hadn't forgotten her irritation when Nat seemed dismissive of Wanda earlier, said crisply, "Wanda has a well-regarded column in the newspaper. Perhaps you've heard of it. She does the horoscopes."

Nat snapped his fingers. "Of course. That's where I've seen you. There's a headshot right next to your column. I'm quite a fan of yours. I never miss your column."

Wanda's blush deepened and she studied her feet. "Thank yew."

Myrtle said, "I'm surprised someone your age reads the newspaper at all."

"The entire reason I subscribe is for Wanda. I'd love to have a reading with you."

Myrtle quickly interjected. "There's a fee for that." She could feel rather defensive on Wanda's behalf. Readings could be very tiring, and she certainly didn't want Wanda to be taken advantage of. Especially by this slick, wealthy-looking young man.

"Of course. I've got cash with me." He glanced at his watch again. "You know what? I'll cancel the meeting. There's a small sitting area that's usually pretty quiet inside town hall. Would now work for you?"

Wanda looked at Myrtle, then nodded.

"I'll come along, too," said Myrtle. If Nat Drake was a potential murderer, she certainly wasn't going to leave Wanda alone with him.

The sitting area was modest, but then the town hall was modest, as was Bradley itself. Myrtle was curious how this completely off-the-cuff reading was going to transpire. Wanda's other readings were usually at her home, where she had things like tarot cards, a crystal ball, and tea leaves.

Then Wanda, almost apologetically, reached for Nat's hand. He stuck it out, peering at her as she peered at his palm. Wanda's eyes flickered uneasily.

"Something wrong?" asked Nat sharply.

Wanda had told Myrtle before that no one wanted to hear anything bad. Why would they? Wanda's hesitation made Nat add, "Go ahead and tell me what you see."

Wanda said, "Money. And unhappiness." She didn't meet his eyes.

Nat sighed, nodding. "Anything else?"

Wanda put down his hand and folded her arms, closing her eyes. Nat and Myrtle looked on as she sat silently, almost as if she were listening. Then she opened her eyes. She cleared her throat. "Kale smoothies."

Myrtle thought perhaps poor Wanda had suffered a minor stroke. But Nat immediately laughed. "My ex-girlfriend, Trisha. She drinks two of those things a day. I'm considering trying to get back together with her. I was going to call her today and ask her out to dinner."

"Don't," drawled Wanda.

Nat nodded, looking thoughtful. "I won't. Thank you."

That was all Wanda could see, so minutes later, Wanda was slowly driving Myrtle back home. Wanda looked pale and tired, as she often did after a reading.

"Do you want to come in and have a nap for a while?" asked Myrtle with concern.

Wanda shook her head. "Think I'll head home. Work in th' yard."

Myrtle nodded. That was always very restorative for Wanda. She loved her plants. Although she wasn't sure how much was growing in February. She supposed there was always pruning to do. "Oh, I know what I've been meaning to tell you. Garden club is tomorrow. How about you come along?"

Wanda gave her a grin. "You wanna go because Ollie will be there."

"Your psychic abilities are truly stupendous today. Yes, Teddy's former employee will be speaking to the group. Maybe I can get Miles to attend, too. He does enjoy going to some meetings."

Wanda pulled carefully into Myrtle's driveway, then gave her a reproachful look. "Gotta be careful around Miles now."

"Yes, I know. He's sad. But perhaps, if he has activities to do, he'll be a bit better." Myrtle was quickly tiring of treating Miles with kid gloves.

Wanda appeared doubtful at this. "Mebbe yew should put yer feet up, too."

"Me? I'm absolutely fine."

But thirty minutes later, Myrtle was asleep on her sofa, Pasha curled up next to her.

Chapter Nine

When she awakened from her nap, she immediately started thinking about Imogen Winthrop, the new copyeditor. Perhaps she'd been dreaming about her. If so, it would explain the mood Myrtle had woken up in. She decided to pay a visit and walk over to Imogen's house. It wouldn't be a short walk, but she felt she could use the opportunity to stretch her legs. She grabbed a loaf of Elaine's "bread" and stuck it into a tote bag, feeling its weight as she walked.

Myrtle knew Imogen well enough to recognize the rebellious streak hiding under her elderly exterior. Her contrarian nature was as predictable as it was frustrating. However, Myrtle also realized it could be a tool.

A direct approach, trying to dissuade Imogen from joining the *Bradley Bugle*, would likely backfire spectacularly. Imogen would probably dig her heels in, more determined than ever to work for the newspaper. The solution, Myrtle reasoned, was to flip the script. Instead of discouraging Imogen, she'd feign enthusiasm.

It might be a delicate balance, however. Push too hard, and Imogen might see through the ruse. She wasn't a stupid woman.

To refine her strategy further, Myrtle decided she'd judiciously sprinkle in some cons to working at the *Bugle*. These wouldn't necessarily be outright negatives, but subtle hints at potential drawbacks. She'd mention them casually, almost as afterthoughts, knowing Imogen would latch onto the breadcrumbs of doubt and nurture them into full-blown objections.

Myrtle walked up a cobblestone path lined with precisely trimmed boxwood hedges to Imogen's cheery cottage, plastering a big, fake smile on her face. The small, white clapboard house sat behind a meticulously manicured lawn, surrounded by a stereotypical white picket fence. The front door was a robin's egg blue with a brass door knocker polished to a mirror-like shine. Myrtle banged on the door, ignoring the knocker.

A small woman, Imogen looked somewhat larger due to not only her rigid posture but also her perfectly coiffed silver bouffant, which added several extra inches to her height. She looked at Myrtle impassively, her pale blue eyes magnified behind cat-eye glasses. Imogen was wearing a crisp blouse with a cameo brooch, a string of pearls, and pink slacks. Somehow, she looked much older than Myrtle, despite being significantly Myrtle's junior.

"Imogen!" squealed Myrtle, leaping forward to give Imogen a hug with the arm that wasn't carrying her cane and the tote bag with the loaf of bread.

Imogen looked startled, as well as she might. It was most unlike Myrtle to squeal and equally unlike her to hug. "Myrtle," she said with a gasp.

Myrtle maneuvered her way inside the small house. "I brought you some homemade bread." She purposefully omitted the part that it wasn't homemade by Myrtle herself. "I've heard from Sloan that you're on the team. I couldn't be more delighted."

Imogen was still looking rather stunned. But now her expression was moving more into the territory of skepticism, as if she was being presented with a poorly written essay she'd been tasked to grade. "Delighted?"

"Positively elated. As a veteran journalist, I'm so happy to welcome you aboard. The paper is in dire need of copyediting, you know."

This Imogen agreed with. "The newspaper's editing is in horrid shape. Horrid."

"I'm sure you'll be fixing the problem immediately. It's very self-sacrificing of you to take a project of this magnitude on."

Imogen frowned. "Magnitude? It's a local newspaper."

"Indeed it is. That's why it's such a big undertaking. You see, with a small-town newspaper, stories happen quite spontaneously. You'll have to make sure every name is correct before it's printed. People in Bradley get extremely upset if their name is misprinted in the paper. *Extremely.*" Myrtle gave a cheery chuckle.

Imogen said slowly, "Of course. That would be natural."

"You won't believe the number of articles that get added at the end of the day. I understand from Sloan that you'll be making the trip over to the *Bugle* instead of editing online."

Imogen nodded. "I don't have a computer."

"That's very good of you to take that extra step. I do hope you have your chiropractor on speed dial, though." Myrtle's eyes twinkled merrily. "The office chairs haven't been replaced in decades."

Apparently, the late-day visits to the newsroom were weighing heavily on Imogen. She said, "About the articles that come in late. What sorts of things are we talking about? Important breaking news?"

"If you call 'High School Marching Band's Bake Sale Raises Funds for New Tubas' an important breaking news story," said Myrtle with a shrug. "The parents of the high school students certainly do. You'll be fact-checking the spelling of every single name. And Sloan is always mindful of newspaper sales, so he mentions as many names as he possibly can so the doting parents will buy multiple copies of the paper." Myrtle hoped she wasn't laying it on too thick.

Imogen's thin, perfectly arched eyebrows drew together, creating a series of fine wrinkles across her forehead. The corners of her mouth turned sharply downward, forming deep parentheses around her lips.

Myrtle didn't want to overdo things. Better to give Imogen more downsides of working for the *Bugle* in future visits. Because she planned on future visits. "I'd better let you go. You'll need to rest up for your newspaper adventure! Enjoy the bread—I'll bring more by the next time I come."

"The next time?"

"Of course," said Myrtle. "Since we're colleagues now."

THE REST OF THE DAY was noneventful, and the following morning, Myrtle was up bright and early. Luckily, her lengthy nap the day before hadn't been long enough to mess up her sleep that night. She was pleasantly surprised when she slept through the night and woke up at the late-for-Myrtle time of five-thirty.

After consuming a large breakfast similar to the one yesterday, Myrtle set about doing her crossword puzzle. Then she read the comics. Afterwards, she felt sustained enough to tackle the front-page news. She quickly discovered the front-page news was not at all appealing and did the sudoku, instead.

Finally, the sun was up and the yard was bathed in a warm glow. She very much wanted to weed around the mailbox. Her yardman, Dusty, had done a pitiful job with the weed whacking lately. Myrtle frowned, realizing she also wanted him to come drag her extensive gnome collection into the front yard. After her conversation with Red yesterday at town hall, he deserved to have a full display. She smiled at the thought of how irritated he'd be.

"Dusty?" asked Myrtle in a peremptory tone on the phone.

"Whaa? What time is it?" asked a groggy Dusty.

"It feels like it's practically noon. Let's see. It's eight-thirty."

"I done mowed yer grass last week, Miz Myrtle! It ain't growed since then."

"As it happens, I agree with you this time. I don't think the grass has grown very much in a week. It's likely dormant since it's winter."

Dusty howled, "Then why're you buggin' me?"

"I'm bugging you because I want you to pull my gnomes out. There's been an infraction."

Dusty sounded curious. "What's he done now?"

"He's been very annoying. He suggested I sleep more and join a sittercize class."

Dusty gave a chortling laugh. "Bet that didn't go down well."

"It did not. So, gnomes?"

"Reckon I could put 'em out."

Myrtle frowned. This was not the eager response to her call for action that she'd hoped for. "Today?"

Some muttering occurred on the other end of the line.

"Now?" prompted Myrtle.

Dusty sighed. "Reckon I'm awake now."

"Excellent. I find I get better results with Red when it's a matter of cause and effect. He does something maddening and the gnomes come out. If there's too much delay, it really loses its punch."

Dusty grunted in response. Then he put the phone down. He was nearly as irritating as Red was. She didn't feel at all bad about waking him. Puddin had blamed her poor performance at baseboard cleaning on Dusty's snoring, after all. It hadn't put Dusty in Myrtle's good graces.

Also very irritating, of course, was Myrtle's next-door neighbor, Erma. She'd had a delightful reprieve from Erma recently, which meant she feared her luck was at an end. And she'd forgotten to ask Dusty to weed-whack around the mailbox, which meant it was going to bother her until she took care of it. She decided to use her hoe instead of kneeling to pull the weeds. That way, she could use the hoe instead of her cane. Myrtle really wanted to expedite the weeds' removal. She simply didn't feel right going to garden club with the area surrounding her mailbox in such poor condition.

Myrtle peeked out the front door, looking warily about to see if Erma was lurking. Not spotting her, she hurried to the mailbox. Erma's yard looked even worse than it had before. She'd tried to pull off a yard makeover recently, and it had gone horribly wrong. Myrtle never thought she'd feel nostalgic over Erma's weeds. But the weeds had been *green*, at least. They were much better than the horrid red clay wasteland now situated next door.

Myrtle started hacking away at the crabgrass and clover around the mailbox. She stopped to catch her breath and saw Pasha padding down the driveway. Pasha stopped, swishing her tail, and sat down, facing Erma's, a determined air about her.

Myrtle beamed at her. "Good girl!" Erma was terribly allergic to cats and scurried away like the rat she resembled whenever Pasha was around. With Pasha protecting her, Myrtle finished with her weeding in record time.

"Want to come inside and eat?" asked Myrtle when she caught up with the black cat in the driveway.

But Pasha apparently didn't fancy anything to eat. Instead, she looked up at Myrtle, purred, and then bounded off for other adventures.

Inside the house, Myrtle checked the time. By now it was after nine o'clock. That seemed a very reasonable time to call Miles and ask him if he'd like to go to garden club. Surely, he couldn't still be sleeping.

But he was. Miles answered the phone in a very sleepy voice. "Myrtle? What is it?"

"Gracious, are you still asleep? I've been up for hours."

"I've no doubt," said Miles, sounding irritated. "I, however, haven't."

Myrtle said, "I wanted to see if you'd like to go to garden club today. Wanda is coming along. Ollie is going to be the speaker."

Miles didn't say anything, which Myrtle took as confusion over who Ollie was. "Ollie used to work with Teddy, remember? Teddy allegedly fired him, which makes Ollie an excellent suspect."

Miles said, "I think I'll pass on garden club, Myrtle. I wasn't planning on having that lively of a day today."

"Garden club is lively? It's quite staid compared to book club. Now *book* club can be lively, especially if Blanche is hosting it. Alcohol makes those ladies very capricious. But garden club is never that way." Myrtle paused. "If garden club is out, how about if you come over to watch *Tomorrow's Promise* with me?"

Miles demurred. "I don't know. The storyline has gotten kind of silly."

"Silly? The plot is *always* silly. That's what makes watching it so much fun."

"Just the same, I think I'll pass. Tell Wanda hi for me." And Miles rang off.

Chapter Ten

Wanda picked up Myrtle in the early afternoon for garden club. Myrtle was still grumbling about Miles. Wanda shrugged. "Don't worry about it. Mebbe he needs time."

"I can't imagine why. He's retired. All he *has* is time. It's all very irritating."

But when they arrived at Tippy's house for the garden club meeting, Myrtle managed to put Miles's odd behavior behind her for the afternoon. Tippy, as usual, had gone all out. Her house was a picturesque white house with grand columns and a sprawling verandah dotted with rocking chairs. She had hanging baskets with vibrant flowers on the verandah, giving a splash of color against the white backdrop.

Tippy set up the meeting area under a large, shady magnolia. Either Tippy or someone who worked for her had set out folding chairs with floral cushions in two semi-circles facing a lectern where Ollie Spearman would speak. Most of the women were gathered around a long table with a crisp white tablecloth, which was adorned with small vases of fresh-cut flowers from Tippy's garden. Refreshments, including pitchers of iced tea and lemonade and finger sandwiches and cookies, were laid out on the table.

Myrtle muttered to Wanda, "Trust Tippy to have picked the perfect day for an outdoor garden club meeting. I can't imagine planning something like this for February. If *I'd* done that, it would have been sleeting or some such nonsense."

"Yep," agreed Wanda. She was eyeing the finger sandwiches hungrily. Myrtle wasn't in the slightest bit hungry, but she knew Wanda well enough to realize she wouldn't touch the food unless Myrtle was with her.

"Let's eat," said Myrtle. "I'm starving."

Minutes later, Myrtle steered them to the seats, picked two, and sat down. If they milled around too much, Wanda would be pestered for fortunes from the garden club gaggle. They'd flutter around like a flock of over-dressed hens, clucking at Wanda as if she were a carnival sideshow. Everyone seemed to over-dress when Tippy was hosting. Myrtle looked at her plain pants and sweater with satisfaction. Wanda was dressed in similar garb.

"What's up with this Ollie?" asked Wanda quietly.

"Well, I'm curious to hear him speak. Apparently, Teddy thought him too avant-garde for the town of Bradley. He's supposed to talk about flower arranging. But the main reason I wanted to be here is to speak with him afterward. Teddy stole his girlfriend, then fired him. He can't have been happy about that."

"Mad enough to kill somebody?" asked Wanda.

"That's what we need to find out." Myrtle nibbled at her pimento cheese finger sandwich. She noticed Wanda had already finished a medley of chicken salad, egg salad, and tuna salad sandwiches. Fortunately, she had piled her plate, despite her lack of appetite. "My eyes were bigger than my stomach," she said, loading Wanda's plate surreptitiously with food.

Wanda gave her a knowing look, but happily took the food.

Tippy suddenly swooped down on them, playing the hostess. It was a role she was exceedingly good at. "Good to see you both here! Wanda, that color looks beautiful on you."

Wanda looked down with surprise to see what she was wearing. It was a dark purple sweater. She gave Tippy a gap-toothed grin. "Thanks, Tippy."

"Are y'all excited about the speaker?" asked Tippy.

Wanda nodded. Myrtle tilted her head to one side. "Is Ollie someone we should be excited about?"

Tippy frowned. "He has very impressive credentials, which I'll be touching on when I introduce him."

Myrtle raised her eyebrows. "Credentials? I didn't really realize florists had them. They seem to be more for real estate agents, doctors, and stylists."

"Well, they're for florists, too. Ollie has his CFDA."

Myrtle scowled at the acronym. She was never a fan of people using acronyms without explaining them first. It was all very annoying.

Tippy caught her look. "He's a certified floral design associate. It's from the National Career Certification Board. Not only that, but he completed an advanced program from the Floral Design Institute. Plus, he's been published in several floral design magazines."

"Mercy," muttered Myrtle. "He certainly does have credentials." She wondered why he'd chosen to live in a small town, which had little need for multiple florists.

"He does. But, as you know, he's gone through a rather tough time lately. I thought he'd be the perfect person to speak at our February meeting. We'll be a nice distraction for him."

Myrtle said, "Yes, he's had a rough time. What have you heard about him and Teddy?"

Tippy hesitated, her proper demeanor warring with her desire to share information. She glanced around, ensuring they were alone, then leaned in slightly. The temptation to be the source of coveted information, to hold court with the latest news, proved too strong for even her usual decorum. Her voice lowered to a conspiratorial whisper, a hint of excitement gleaming in her eyes.

"Well, I normally don't indulge in idle gossip, you understand," Tippy began, her tone suggesting she was about to do exactly that. "But given the circumstances, and since I know you're trying to do a bit of sleuthing, I suppose it won't do any harm. I understood from Ollie that he feels very guilty about not parting with Teddy on good terms. You just never know when a conversation with someone will end up being your last, do you? Something we should all keep in mind." Tippy glanced over at the long table. "Excuse me, it looks like my refreshments might need refreshing." She laughed at her turn of phrase. "See you later, ladies. Enjoy the speaker."

A few minutes later, Tippy was introducing Ollie, repeating the acronyms, and generally giving a very obsequious introduction. The ladies applauded politely as a man in his mid-forties with a well-groomed salt-and-pepper beard stepped up to the lectern. Myrtle thought he looked a little tired. Tippy might be convinced garden club was just the distraction Ollie needed, but Myrtle wondered if the prep work for speaking might have been a little too much.

Ollie cleared his throat and seemed to consult some note cards. "Thanks so much for hosting me today. Thanks especially to Tippy." He glanced around. "What a lovely yard you have. Just beautiful, even in February." He cast his gaze around the yard. "Let's see. I spot camellias, hellebores, winter jasmine, and pansies." He gave Tippy a wry look. "I'm suddenly feeling like I need to spruce up my own yard."

The ladies tittered at this. Ollie continued his talk, starting with "blooms and balance," discussing the apparently delicate balance in floral arrangements where the colors, shapes, and textures must harmonize.

Myrtle might have grown just the tiniest bit sleepy when he moved onto "the language of petals" and the symbolism between different flowers. But Wanda was listening attentively when Ollie described daffodils as symbolizing new beginnings and forget-me-nots for memories. Ollie finished up his talk by saying, "Finally, I'd like to invite all of you to do one thing. You all clearly love flowers and nature. Go out in it. Do it every single day. I leave my house every morning at dawn, pull on my boots, and take a walk through the woods and out by the lake. I keep my muddy boots right outside the front door to make it easier for me. That's my advice to you—make it easy to run out and enjoy nature. No matter what problems come up during my day, I know I've started it well and with serenity. Thank you."

Then Ollie invited questions from the audience. The ladies seemed to be quite taken with him, and peppered him with questions involving budget-friendly arranging, the best tools to use, how best to transport arrangements without damaging them, and using unusual containers. Myrtle was antsy during this section of the talk. She had the feeling the garden club gaggle was just enjoying hearing their own voices. Or perhaps they were simply wanting to engage with the attractive Ollie.

Finally, things wrapped up, and the applause was very warm. Ollie gave a small bow and a smile and stepped away from the lectern. He was, of course, immediately surrounded by the ladies, who all appeared to have more questions.

"We might be here a while," said Myrtle grimly.

"It's okay," said Wanda.

After about twenty minutes, the huddle around Ollie Spearman dissipated, and Myrtle and Wanda stepped up to talk. He smiled at them, fully expecting to be talking about flower arrangements or perhaps other floral topics. Myrtle introduced herself and Wanda, however, then jumped right into the topic at the forefront of her mind.

"We wanted to tell you how sorry we were about Teddy," said Myrtle. "A friend of mine and I found him. Such a terrible tragedy."

Ollie took a reflexive step back, as if wanting to disengage from them and their inconvenient interest in murder. "Yes. Yes, it was."

"I understand that you might have left Blossom Serenade recently." She paused, hoping he would fill in the blanks in his own words.

"That's correct," he said. He was giving Myrtle and Wanda somewhat leery looks, unsure where the conversation was heading.

Myrtle was making it up as she went along. But she thought she might have an approach that would work well with Ollie. "Actually, I was at Teddy's shop on assignment. I'm a reporter for the *Bradley Bugle*," Myrtle explained, her tone casual yet professional. "It got me thinking that your new venture could make for an interesting story. Our readers would love to hear about a local entrepreneur like yourself." She tilted her head, curiosity evident in her voice. "I'm not entirely clear on your current setup though. Have you opened a physical storefront, or are you operating from home?"

It had clearly been the right approach. Ollie brightened as soon as Myrtle mentioned the newspaper. Promo was always helpful for new businesses. "I *don't* have a physical storefront right now, no. But I'm working on finding a place."

Wanda drawled, "Seems like a place jest opened up."

Ollie gave her a curious look. "Well, that's certainly true. Although I'm not sure I'd want to move to the Blossoms and Serenade building. It's full of a lot of memories, you know. Maybe it would be good to start a new place from scratch."

"That makes sense," said Myrtle. "Word on the street is that you and Teddy didn't part under the most amicable terms. Working in a place with such negative memories wouldn't be the right way to move forward."

Ollie looked taken aback. "Oh, I don't know that I'd say our parting wasn't amicable. Business relationships, like any others, go through their ups and downs." He frowned. "Is this off-the-record?"

"Naturally. I'll take out my notepad if I'm jotting down quotes. My memory is excellent, but it's not *that* good."

"Okay," said Ollie. "It's true that I left Blossom Serenade before I probably should have. I didn't have anything else lined up. I didn't have a plan or a place to do my business. I didn't even have any flowers," he said ruefully.

Myrtle said, "Did Teddy let you go?" Because that's what people had been saying.

"Absolutely not. I quit the shop voluntarily. Teddy and I had creative differences. I wanted exciting new arrangements, something that brought real artistry into the process. Teddy was more pedestrian, wanting to just make something small. Something commercial that would sell right away to some guy who just needed a bouquet to tell his wife he was sorry for not putting his dishes in the dishwasher for the millionth time."

Wanda looked doubtful. Myrtle silently agreed with her. She didn't believe Ollie was telling the truth. "I see," said Myrtle. "I understood there was also friction because Teddy was dating someone who'd been your girlfriend."

An undefinable look flashed over Ollie's features for a moment. A mix of sadness and anger, perhaps? It was gone before Myrtle could properly analyze it. Then he said in an admiring tone, "You *are* a good reporter, aren't you? But you've gotten the wrong end of the stick for that one. Linda and I parted amicably, then Teddy asked if he might invite her out to dinner." He shrugged. "It wasn't the big, romantic drama that the town of Bradley hoped it might be."

Ollie frowned and added slowly, "But if the town of Bradley *thinks* that's what happened, and they think I'm a murderer, I really do need to have a nice feature in the paper, don't I?"

"I think a feature on you and your business would show the town you're not hiding anything. That you're utterly trustworthy. And it would help if we had some stunning pictures of your arrangements. And perhaps a nice photo of you looking completely innocuous."

Ollie nodded eagerly. "Let's do that. I originally was thinking the article should come out as soon as possible, but it would be better if we had good pictures. Could you come to my place another day for the photos of arrangements?"

"Of course." Myrtle paused. "Although it might be nice to take a picture of you today. The weather is beautiful, Tippy's garden is lovely, and you're all dressed up for your speaking engagement."

"Good point." Ollie started looking around him through narrowed eyes, trying to determine a location with good light. "How about over there?"

Myrtle and Wanda followed him over to a tall, blooming camellia bush. While he posed, looking awkward, Myrtle carefully took pictures of him with her cell phone. She was a competent photographer, although not very confident in her abilities with the medium. Which would explain why she snapped photos for the next five minutes.

Finally, she decided she must have a good picture in the bunch. "I'm sure one of these will work well. I'll call you later on to set up a date to take photos of your flowers."

"Perfect." Ollie looked a little worried. "I'm still concerned about the public's reaction to Teddy's death and how it might affect my business. I know that sounds petty."

"That's a completely valid concern. I believe this profile on you will have the desired effect."

Ollie nodded. "This whole thing is sad in so many ways. I know I said Teddy created pedestrian arrangements, but he was extremely talented. He just didn't care to showcase that talent. But he always seemed to know exactly what a customer was looking for. Teddy was very intuitive as a florist. I'm just sorry that we didn't part on the best of terms. Now we don't have the opportunity to bridge our differences and be friends again. That was stolen from us."

"You was friends," croaked Wanda.

Ollie looked at her with surprise, as if he'd forgotten she was there. "That's right. We spent countless late nights at Blossom Serenade. We'd argue about designs, sip lukewarm coffee, and rearrange vases. I'm really struggling to grasp the fact he's gone forever."

Myrtle said, "You spent a lot of time with Teddy, so you must have known a lot about what was going on in his life. Who do you think might have done this to him?"

Ollie shrugged helplessly again. "I'd feel like I'd be throwing someone under the bus by saying anything."

"This is still off-the-record."

"Well, I don't like to speak ill of anyone, but since you're asking... Teddy had his share of conflicts. His sister Zoey, for instance—she's quite a handful. Always showing up unannounced, demanding money. Teddy was at his wit's end with her. The last time I saw her, I overheard them having a terrible row. Something about her 'ruining everything' again. Zoey treated Teddy as if he were her last lifeline. He'd been bailing her out for years, but lately, he'd started refusing. Said he couldn't enable her anymore. Zoey didn't take it well. She threatened to sell some old family heirlooms if Teddy didn't help her. It was getting ugly."

Myrtle asked, "Did she? Sell the heirlooms, I mean?"

"Zoey sure did. Teddy wasn't too happy about that, but what could he do?"

Ollie paused, as if reluctant to continue, but feeling compelled to do so.

"And then there's Nat Drake, the developer. He and Teddy were constantly butting heads over that land deal."

Myrtle nodded. "The salamander."

"Teddy was determined to save the salamander. But that wasn't the only issue. You know that development was going to be abutting Teddy's property. He was dead set against it, saying it would destroy the town's character. Nat didn't take kindly to the opposition. Nat looked furious, told Teddy he'd 'regret getting in his way.'"

Myrtle and Wanda glanced at each other. Myrtle said, "Do you think Nat did something about it?"

Ollie shrugged. "It's not like Teddy's death meant the development could move forward. The endangered animal is still in that stream. But Nat might have murdered Teddy out of revenge." He shook his head sadly. "It's awful to think about, really. Teddy had his flaws, but he didn't deserve this. I just hope they find out who did it soon."

Myrtle affected an innocent, merely nosy-old-lady expression. "Were Teddy and Linda happy together?"

"Teddy had actually broken things off with Linda a few weeks ago."

Myrtle opened her eyes wide. "Mercy. Do you think Linda could possibly have been involved? That she might have been upset at Teddy and acted out?"

Ollie immediately shook his head. "No, no, that wouldn't have been like Linda at all. She was always a very rational person. I mean, she owns her own business, so she can't be the kind of person to fly off the handle. Besides, she and Teddy weren't meant for each other. Their personalities were very different. I'm sure Linda sensed that. I can't imagine Linda being devastated when her relationship with Teddy ended."

"Teddy and Linda didn't get along well?" asked Myrtle.

Ollie rubbed his forehead as if it were hurting. "Well, it seemed to me like they argued over just about everything. They were very different people in many ways. Teddy was more inclined to quiet evenings at home. Linda was a lot more outgoing and wanted them to hang out with friends. I mean, these were just silly, minor differences, but they tended to blow up into really big issues."

"So they just weren't very compatible."

"Bingo," said Ollie. "They'd argue over dumb things, too. Foods they liked, movie choices, even the type of coffee they'd drink. But you know, these little disagreements really rankled them. I think it was because they were such different people. Linda wanted to have these open conversations about any problems they had, while Teddy was more reserved and didn't want to hash over relationship stuff."

"It sounds like the two of them weren't particularly suited to one another," said Myrtle. "Although they do say opposites attract."

Ollie was quiet for a moment. "Linda and I were actually a lot more compatible. We had a good deal in common, including our backgrounds. We were both from modest backgrounds, the first in our families to go to college. We liked a lot of the same things. When we had our amicable breakup I mentioned before, I always felt we would end up back together again. That maybe we just needed a break."

Myrtle said, "Oh, isn't that nice? How lovely that the two of you might be a couple again."

Ollie gave her a wry look. "Well, it's not a done deal yet. I've been trying to reach out to Linda, but I think she's been busy. I wanted to tell her I was sorry about Teddy, of course. But I also wanted to invite her to a concert that's being held at the community center soon. Something I thought we might both enjoy."

"I hope it works out," said Myrtle.

As Myrtle was about to continue her probing, a familiar voice suddenly cut through the air, causing her to stiffen. Those saccharine, affected tones could only belong to one person.

"Now, Myrtle! You and Wanda shouldn't monopolize poor Ollie's time," Erma Sherman cooed from behind them, her words dripping with false sweetness. Myrtle had never heard Erma coo and hoped never to again. "I've been simply dying to ask him about my yard."

Myrtle turned, barely suppressing a grimace. Erma stood there, beaming with self-importance, a stack of photographs clutched in her grubby hands.

At first, Ollie's face registered relief at the interruption, clearly grateful for a reprieve from Myrtle's relentless questioning about the murder. However, his expression quickly transformed as Erma launched into a detailed account of her landscaping woes, thrusting photo after photo of her ravaged garden under his nose.

Ollie's initial polite interest gave way to barely concealed horror. His eyes widened, and he recoiled slightly as he flipped through the images, each one seemingly worse than the last. It was as if he were watching a particularly gruesome scene in a horror film, unable to look away from the botanical carnage Erma had wrought.

Chapter Eleven

Myrtle and Wanda climbed into Wanda's car. "That Erma," said Myrtle. "Who brings actual printed photographs instead of showing them on a phone? And I swear she crawls out of the woodwork. I thought everybody had left garden club except for Tippy."

Wanda shook her head. "Saw her talkin' to Tippy."

"No doubt trying to figure out how to make her pitiful yard look as good as Tippy's does."

Wanda said, "Tippy's yard is real good."

"Sure, it is. And if you and I had Tippy's money, ours would look just as nice." Myrtle made a face. "Sorry for the vitriol. I do like Tippy, even if she annoys me sometimes. But we were having such a good interview with Ollie before Erma inserted herself into our conversation."

Wanda carefully drove down the street at about ten miles an hour. Someone rode her bumper, and she tilted up the rear-view mirror so she couldn't see them or any unpleasant hand gestures they might make. "Reckon we still got good info."

"Yes, I suppose you're right. Although much of the information we got was probably lies. I strongly suspect that just about everything that came out of Ollie's mouth was a falsehood of some kind. I've heard he was fired and that he was devastated when his relationship with Linda was over. He told us he left of his own volition and was fine with Teddy dating his old girl-friend." Myrtle shrugged.

Wanda turned down Myrtle's street. "Reckon he's wantin' to protect himself. Don't want to look like a killer."

"You're right, of course. But it's all very annoying. These murder investigations would be over in no time if people simply told the truth."

Wanda pulled into Myrtle's driveway, but didn't seem to be turning off the car or preparing to go inside. "You'll come in and visit for a while, won't you?" asked Myrtle.

Wanda shook her head, giving her a grin. "Nope. Yer gonna play with yer gran'baby. See ya later."

Myrtle waved as she backed out of her driveway. Sure enough, Elaine and Jack came right outside with a container of bubbles. Elaine waved her over, and Jack gave her a big hug.

"How about if I blow bubbles for Jack for a few minutes while you do whatever it is you need to do?" offered Myrtle.

Elaine grinned at her. "You're spoiling me. As it is, I do need to make a couple of phone calls. I've got to schedule a dental cleaning for Red and call a friend with an RSVP. Thanks!"

She dashed off, and Myrtle happily blew bubbles. She was apparently making all the wrong kinds, though, because Jack said, "*Big* bubbles, Nana!"

Myrtle then discovered if she blew slowly, the bubbles grew larger. This went on for some time. Myrtle felt as if she'd gone into respiratory therapy by the end of the bubble fun. Jack, of course, was having the time of his life, chasing bubbles in the front yard, trying to hold them, and getting soapy bubbles all over himself.

Elaine came back out a few minutes later. "Ready for a snack?" she asked Jack. Jack nodded enthusiastically, and Elaine handed him a bag of graham crackers with peanut butter.

"We had fun!" said Jack.

"Indeed we did," said Myrtle. "Especially after I figured out how to get bubbles with larger circumferences."

Elaine said, "Talking about figuring things out, did you make headway with the bread starter?"

Myrtle shook her head. "Not yet. I got distracted by making a casserole for Zoey Hartfield."

There was an expression on Elaine's face that Myrtle couldn't quite read. "Did you? What did you cook?"

"Paprika chicken. Except I substituted cayenne."

Elaine's inscrutable expression deepened. Myrtle wondered if perhaps she was sad that she hadn't tried to use the bread starter. A sad Elaine was something she decidedly couldn't handle today. Not with a morose Miles on top of it all. "You know, I think I'll get right on that bread starter. You've inspired me."

"Oh, well, there's plenty of time. You've been very busy lately."

Myrtle said cheerfully, "There's always time for something new and exciting to try." If bread could indeed be classified that way.

She heard a car turn onto the street, glanced up, and saw it was Red's police cruiser. "And there's no time like the present," Myrtle added. "See you two later." She hurried across the street, cane thumping, trying to get inside before Red spotted her and hollered at her again for showing up at the town hall development meeting.

Sadly, her speedy departure had already been witnessed. A minute later, her doorbell rang.

Myrtle stomped to her front door, uncharitable thoughts about her son in her head. He stood glowering at her on her doorstep.

"Well, come on in. You can help me in the kitchen. Elaine gave me some bread starter."

Red muttered, "Why on earth did she do that?"

"I suppose she has too much of it. I understand you have bread coming out of your ears."

Red followed his mother into the kitchen. "Yeah. And it's the hardest bread you've ever seen."

"I couldn't help but notice a loaf of Elaine's bread was at the crime scene." Myrtle looked in her pantry to find something to put in the bread starter. She frowned at her limited options.

"Now, I don't want that leaking out, Mama. That's sensitive information."

Myrtle turned around to look at Red. "Sensitive because you don't want details from Teddy's murder to come out? Elaine is already aware you left her bread there. I suppose you were trying to unload as many loaves as possible."

"Correct. I don't want information regarding the crime scene to be released," growled Red. "And for your information, forensics has determined her bread wasn't used in the crime. It was solely the glass vase. Which, also does not need to be disclosed."

"I wouldn't dream of telling anyone." Myrtle sniffed.

"And while we're having this lovely conversation, I want to give you a warning."

"Here we go," said Myrtle.

"Don't get involved in this case. I know how intrigued you get over this stuff. I don't want you sticking in your nose where it doesn't belong."

"Where *do* you think my nose belongs? In sittercize class?"

Red rolled his eyes. "I saw what you thought of that suggestion when your gnomes appeared in the yard. But yes, I do think sittercize would be a great idea. There are plenty of nice ladies and a couple of great gentlemen in the class."

"Like who?" asked Myrtle suspiciously.

"People you know."

"That doesn't help. I know just about everybody in this town," said Myrtle.

"Okay, well, how about Marcia Tolly? She's in the class. And everybody thinks she's delightful."

"A delightful what? A delightful pain? Because she is."

Red said, "You know, Mama, people might describe you as a delightful pain, yourself."

"They wouldn't dare." Myrtle pulled out some chocolate chips and marshmallows absently. "Thinking back to the crime scene, was there any physical evidence available? Fingerprints? Hair? Other things?"

"You can't think I'm going to give you that information."

Myrtle scowled. "If you did, then I'd be able to write these articles for the paper remotely. I wouldn't have to attend town hall meetings or talk with people who knew Teddy."

"That's another thing. You need to leave the crime reporting to the younger staff members. Or Sloan."

"Pish," said Myrtle. "The younger staff members don't know how to write. And don't even get me started on Sloan."

"You're the one who taught him English."

Myrtle said, "Yes, but it clearly didn't take, did it? By the time he got to high school, he was irreparable. That had nothing to do with me. Anyway, the point is that you're practically forcing me to investigate by not sharing details with me. Now I'm having to get out there like those Watergate guys."

"Watergate guys? You mean Woodward and Bernstein?"

"Precisely," said Myrtle.

"Just as long as you're not meeting up in parking garages with Deep Throat."

"Don't be silly," said Myrtle, viciously adding the chocolate chips and marshmallows to the bread starter. "There are no parking decks in Bradley."

She stared at her bread concoction. It seemed as if it needed something to balance out the sweetness. Myrtle looked in her pantry again and pulled out some crunchy peanut butter.

Red looked at the bread starter with concern. "Who's this loaf for?"

"I thought it might be fun for Jack."

"Nope," said Red. "No way. Elaine has Jack eating really healthy stuff right now. This bread isn't going to fit the bill."

"Nonsense. I just saw her give him graham crackers, for heaven's sake. It's not like the boy is subsisting on bean sprouts. He'll love his Nana's bread."

Red said, "I know who you should give the bread to. Miles. He's been looking a little on the scrawny side."

Myrtle considered this. "Actually, I think he has lost a bit of weight, come to think of it. Perhaps I could bring him the loaf."

"Good idea," said Red, relief in his voice. "Now I gotta go. Stay out of this case, Mama."

"Fine," said Myrtle. She'd crossed her fingers before she lied, so it didn't count.

The next morning was a chilly one. Myrtle had baked the bread, and it seemed to be a good deal spongier than Elaine's offerings. No one would confuse it with a murder weapon, that's for sure. She looked at the clock. It was eight-thirty. Miles should certainly be up and about. Myrtle threw on a cardigan sweater and headed out.

And indeed, there was activity at Miles's house. He was in his front yard, looking thoughtfully at a camellia bush that was blooming with gusto. Miles heard the thumping of Myrtle's cane on the sidewalk and turned.

"Good morning!" said Myrtle in a perky tone. She hoped her perkiness would be contagious.

She thought Miles looked a bit more chipper than he had been. Perhaps he'd had a few cups of coffee. "Good morning, Myrtle."

"Problems with the camellia?"

Miles shook his head. "I'm just wondering if I want to deadhead it or wait for more blooms. It seems a little unfair to be doing yard work in February."

"Why not put it off for a week? I'm sure that won't make a difference." Myrtle thrust the tote bag she'd been carrying at Miles. "Here you go."

"What's this?" Miles looked somewhat suspicious.

"It's bread. For you."

Miles jerked backward, away from the bag. "From Elaine?"

"No, no. Don't worry about that. From me. I made the bread."

Now Miles was studying the bag as if it contained an explosive about to detonate. "I'm not sure I need any bread, Myrtle."

"This is better-than-usual bread. I thought a little sugar might sweeten you up."

Miles gave her a tight smile. "Thank you."

"Oh, I remember what I was going to ask you. You were going to check in with your chess friends to find out what Teddy was like when he lost to more advanced players. Did you have the chance to talk with anybody?"

Miles nodded, a thoughtful expression crossing his face. "I had coffee with Frank Holloway. Teddy was always completely mild-mannered with me. But there were some interesting observations from the more skilled players. Frank, our club champion, told me Teddy was a different person when playing at a higher level. He said he became intensely focused, almost aggressive in his style."

Myrtle's eyebrows raised. "Aggressive? That's quite different from your experience."

"Indeed," Miles continued. "Apparently, Teddy didn't take losses well in those matches. He'd analyze the game obsessively afterwards, demanding to know where he went wrong. Some found it off-putting."

"Did Frank mention specific incidents?"

Miles scratched his chin. "Frank told me about what happened after a particularly grueling match with Dr. Simmons. Teddy lost, swept the pieces off the board, and stormed out of the room. It was quite out of character, at least from what I knew of him. I suppose Teddy's competitive nature only emerged when he felt truly tested." Miles paused. "Although I don't really see how this connects with Teddy's death. It seems it would be more important to know that Teddy had anger issues if Teddy were a suspect instead of a victim."

Myrtle said, "I'm wondering if Teddy provoked someone into a sudden, spur-of-the moment attack. Being murdered with a vase seems like an act of passion. What if Teddy blew up at someone like Ollie, Curtis, Nat, Zoey, or Linda? He might have had a sudden flare of fury, prompting the killer to lash out in response."

"I see," said Miles slowly. "That makes sense. I suppose any of them could have responded that way if Teddy acted out."

"It was harder to imagine when you kept saying everybody loved Teddy, and he was such a great guy. If Teddy had a temper, which it seems he did, then his death does appear more plausible." Myrtle paused. "On a similar topic, I also wanted to check in with you and see if you wanted to attend Teddy's memorial service later this morning. Since you and Teddy were friends."

Myrtle could see that Miles was resistant to the idea. But she also knew that Miles was nothing if not courteous and loyal.

There was no way he could purposefully skip Teddy's service, not now that he was aware of it.

"What time?" he asked.

"It's at eleven. Over at the community center. Zoey seems to have thrown it together."

Miles winced. "Has she? Considering the state of her house, I can't imagine her organizing anything. It doesn't seem as if she has many organizational abilities."

"Probably not. We'll have to see what she managed to put together."

Miles nodded, looking a bit apprehensive. "I'll pick you up at 10:30."

Chapter Twelve

Just a couple of hours later, Myrtle and Miles were parking in front of the community center. It was a modest venue with outdated décor and limited facilities. Because it was so generic, it could accommodate lots of different events. This was the first time Myrtle had attended a memorial service there.

Miles's thoughts were running along the same course. "I've never been to a memorial service here. I've been to a town meeting here. And a farmers market."

"Right. And I've been to a couple of bingo nights, a craft fair, and community theater. This is a first."

They walked inside the community center. The service was apparently taking place in the main room of the building, a theater which had a stage and chairs. There was a memorial table by the door on the way into the theater, showcasing snapshots from Teddy's childhood, a few dried flowers, and a candle that appeared to be on the verge of toppling. Zoey had printed some simple programs on her home printer, which seemed to have uneven ink distribution. The font varied wildly from Arial to Comic Sans.

Myrtle and Miles found seats in the theater. Miles murmured, "You'd think there would be lots of flowers at a florist's memorial service."

"Maybe not. After all, the guy who'd formerly created them all is gone."

Miles considered this. "No one thought of Ollie?"

Myrtle shrugged. "This is why Ollie needs a plug in the newspaper. People don't automatically think of him when it's time to come up with an arrangement."

"I'm curious to see what the reception is going to be like," said Miles. "Is it here?"

"Yes. In one of the other rooms." Myrtle sighed. "I'll miss the church ladies doling out their Southern masterpieces."

"My cholesterol level won't miss it," said Miles. "Maybe Zoey will serve something lighter."

"Since Zoey is in such dire straits, I'm imagining there might only be iced tea and lemonade at the reception."

Myrtle was correct. The reception area was adjacent to the theater, separated by a few makeshift partitions. There were only beverages there.

Miles murmured, "The woman over there. She's the one Teddy was dating. She came to some of the chess tournaments with him."

"Ah. Linda Lambert."

Linda was a striking woman in her late-thirties with auburn hair, a flowy black dress, and vintage jewelry.

"We should say hello and give her our condolences. Perhaps I should bake her a loaf of bread. I'll ask Elaine for more bread starter."

Miles shuddered. He appeared to be about to launch into a litany of reasons they shouldn't approach Linda, talk to Linda, or give Linda bread. But Myrtle had already set off in the woman's direction with great determination. Miles grimly followed.

Linda gave them both a tight smile. "Hello there."

Miles introduced himself, and Linda brightened. "Of course. I knew you looked familiar. How are you?"

Miles shook his head. "Well, Teddy's death has been a terrible thing. Are you holding up all right?"

Miles and Linda continued talking like this for a few minutes. Myrtle reached over with her foot and tapped the top of Miles's. He quickly said, "This is my friend, Myrtle Clover."

"You must be Elaine's mother-in-law," said Linda with a smile. "She always says such nice things about you."

"Elaine is a dear," said Myrtle.

"And of course, you're Red's mom."

"I'm afraid so," said Myrtle.

Linda's gaze latched onto Red across the room. He was giving his mother a fed-up look. "I think he's been watching me. Does he believe I killed Teddy?"

Myrtle said, "I'm afraid I'm not acquainted with what goes through Red's mind. But I can tell you from experience that Red always attends memorial services for homicide victims. I'm certain you're not the only person he's keeping an eye on."

Linda nodded, but still looked doubtful. "If I'd only had an alibi," she fretted.

"You didn't?" asked Myrtle.

"Nothing that would keep me from being a suspect. I'm a freelance graphic designer, so it was just a regular workday for me. I was tweaking a digital marketing campaign for a chain of boutiques from home. I'd gotten a last-minute request for promo materials, including social media graphics and email newsletters. Anyway, I was in my home office, totally engrossed in finalizing the details. Nobody can confirm I was there. I only had my cat with me."

Myrtle said, "I see. Well, not everyone has alibis, do they? Especially if they work from home. Did you and Teddy have any special plans?"

"Special plans?" asked Linda blankly.

"For Valentine's Day," said Myrtle. Ollie, of course, had informed her that Teddy had broken things off with Linda prior to the holiday. But Myrtle was curious to see if Linda admitted to the breakup, or whether she didn't mention it.

Miles looked morose again at the mention of Valentine's Day.

"Oh. I think Teddy had some plans up his sleeve. The only problem is that Valentine's Day is his busiest day of the year. We were going to celebrate a couple of days later, instead."

"I'm very sorry about Teddy," said Myrtle. "Miles and I have been thinking about him a lot lately." She went into innocuous little old lady mode. "Such a terrible pity. He seemed like a fine young man. And the two of you must have made a beautiful couple."

Linda gave her a smile. "We had a wonderful relationship. Of course, we were two very different people, but it's almost as if our differences complemented each other. We were always on really good terms and hardly ever argued."

"You were serious then?" asked Myrtle. "Oh, young love."

Linda demurred. "I wouldn't say that Teddy and I were serious, no. There was no talk of marriage or anything like that."

Myrtle nodded. "I see."

Linda said, "It's not that we didn't care for each other. We did. It's more that we were both very busy with our different jobs. We both owned our own business."

Miles cleared his throat. "Small business owners work harder than anyone."

"Very true," agreed Myrtle.

"Exactly," said Linda. "So between the day-to-day work of running a floral business and a graphic design business, dealing with paperwork, and crunching our budgets, we didn't have too much time to think about our future together." She shrugged, looking sad. "I sort of wish we had now."

Myrtle said, "I've heard Teddy had an interest in environmental causes. I thought that was so dear of him."

Miles frowned at her. He apparently believed she was laying it on a bit thick.

"Wasn't it?" asked Linda. "I guess his interest in the environment was a natural development from his interest in floral arranging. He'd been troubled recently by a development near Blossom Serenade that was going to impact an endangered species. Teddy was able to get the development halted."

"Mercy!" said Myrtle. "That's quite a success story. I'd imagine dealing with local government would be tricky to do." She tilted her head curiously. "How did the two of you meet? Are you an activist as well?"

Linda looked uncomfortable, probably because she'd stopped dating one man at Blossom Serenade, only to date another. "I met Teddy through a friend of his."

"Well, that's nice. It's always good when a friend plays matchmaker, isn't it?"

Linda's discomfort deepened. "Yes, it is."

Myrtle shook her head sadly. "Do you have any ideas about who might have been behind this ghastly deed?"

Miles rolled his eyes off to the side.

Linda said slowly, "I've been thinking a lot about that. I mean, I know it wasn't *me*, so who could it have been? And I keep coming back to Zoey. Teddy's sister."

They all glanced across the room at Zoey. She was wearing a black pair of slacks and a black top. Her hair was pulled back in a scrunchie. She looked exhausted and worried.

"Zoey? Did she and Teddy not get along?" asked Miles.

"I guess they got along *okay*, but it wasn't a well-balanced relationship. Teddy was the one who was always giving, and Zoey was always the one who was on the receiving end. Zoey would call, ask for some money from Teddy to get her car repaired, and Teddy would come through and give it to her."

Myrtle said, "That was awfully kind of him."

Linda said wryly, "Kind? I guess it could have been kindness. I always thought it was guilt."

"Whatever would Teddy have to be guilty about?" asked Myrtle. "It sounds as if he should have gotten an award for best brother in Bradley, North Carolina."

"I know. But Teddy felt like he needed to be doing more. His and Zoey's aunt apparently gave Teddy money in her will when she died. But she didn't give anything to Zoey. Zoey was expecting the cash too, counting on it."

Miles said, "That seems very harsh of the aunt."

"It was and it wasn't. Zoey is terrible with money. She'll be the first to tell you that, so I'm not disclosing any family secrets. She'll go into a store for a new bathmat and she'll come out with hundreds of dollars of things that were 'on sale.'" Linda made a face.

This seemed odd to Myrtle. From what she saw of Zoey's house, it was sparsely furnished. Rather spartan-looking on the inside, besides books. It certainly didn't seem to be full of impulse buys or anything expensive. The furniture was practically falling apart. And Myrtle didn't remember seeing an expensive car in the driveway. It made her wonder what Zoey was spending her money on. Or was Linda just exaggerating to make Zoey look bad. Or look more like a suspect.

"That's terrible," said Myrtle. "Teddy must have been worried sick about her."

"He was. And Zoey wouldn't forgive him for receiving their aunt's inheritance and not splitting it with her. She thought he was being unfair. But it was his aunt's wish."

Miles said, "I suppose their aunt realized Zoey wasn't in good financial shape."

"I'm sure she did. From everything I'd heard from Teddy, their aunt was a very sharp woman. It wasn't just that Zoey didn't make good financial decisions, though. She made poor personal decisions, too."

Myrtle said, "Gracious. Has Zoey been in some ill-advised relationships?"

"I'll say. She had a failed marriage that wasn't like a normal divorce. The guy spent money more than Zoey did and also had a drug habit on the side. She was so desperate to get rid of him that she signed whatever divorce paperwork was put in front of her. Her lawyer wasn't that great." Linda shrugged. "And I think Zoey was jealous of Teddy, too. He had a successful business and was in a solid relationship. Maybe she just lost it with him."

Linda froze, glancing somewhere behind Myrtle and Miles. "I should head out. Good seeing both of you." She quickly left.

Myrtle craned her neck to see who Linda had been looking at. She was originally sure it must have been Red. But it appeared to be Ollie Spearman. Ollie was tracking her hasty departure with sad eyes.

Myrtle said, "I don't think Ollie and Linda had an amicable breakup. Regardless of what Ollie might say."

Miles followed her gaze. "No, I don't think so, either. Do you think Ollie murdered Teddy for stealing his girlfriend?"

"Or for firing him? It seems Ollie had plenty of reasons to want Teddy out of the picture."

Miles cast another glance Ollie's way. Ollie was still focused on Linda's exit. "I'm surprised he's here. If he felt that strongly about Teddy, why is he at his memorial service?"

"For appearance's sake, of course. You know how Bradley is. It simply wouldn't do for Ollie to skip Teddy's service. The whole town would be talking. And no one would want to patronize the establishment of a bitter florist."

Miles quirked an eyebrow. "I didn't think that was a prerequisite for being a florist."

"Well, sure. It should be one of those happy businesses. When someone's shopping for flowers, they're wanting a nice, peaceful, pleasant environment."

Miles said, "If you say so. Are we ready to leave, by the way?"

"We should probably speak with Zoey again. Tell her we're sorry about Teddy."

Miles winced. He had the terrible feeling Zoey might have had some of Myrtle's paprika chicken casserole. On the other hand, she was in attendance at the memorial service, so nothing too terrible must have transpired. Although she did look rather pallid.

When they walked up to Zoey, however, she just gave them a tired smile. "Thanks so much for coming," she said in a robotic way, as if her whole being was operating off of muscle memory.

"It was a lovely service," said Myrtle. She was pleased how sincere she sounded. Having attended many, many funerals and memorial services, she was certainly not impressed by this one. But Zoey looked so washed out, so out of it, that Myrtle felt sorry for her.

Miles said, "We'll miss Teddy."

"Yes, I will, too," said Zoey automatically. She gave them a curious look. "Were you talking to Linda just now?"

"We were," said Myrtle. She, naturally, didn't mention that Linda had felt strongly Zoey would make an excellent suspect in her brother's murder.

Zoey frowned. "Linda didn't speak with me."

"Oh, I'm sure she meant to," said Myrtle. "The only problem was that she spotted Ollie. She apparently wanted to avoid him. Linda will likely get in touch with you later for a chat. Are the two of you friends?"

Zoey considered the word "friends" thoughtfully. "No, I guess we weren't, not really. She was Teddy's friend, for sure. Until he ended their relationship. I'm surprised she was here, to be honest. I figured she'd have wanted to put Teddy out of her mind for good."

Yet another witness to confirm that Teddy's relationship with Linda had ended. Myrtle wondered if Linda had told the police that she and Teddy were still dating. It certainly would have minimized her motive in Teddy's murder if their breakup wasn't mentioned.

Someone came up to speak with Zoey, and Myrtle and Miles walked away. Miles said, "I'm glad we're leaving. That whole service had a very weird vibe. Didn't you think?"

"It was unusual. I thought at first it was because of the venue and how shabby the place was, which was surely not Zoey's fault. But I think now that it has to do with Zoey. Did it seem to you like she was just really out of it?"

They climbed into Miles's sedan. He said, "It did seem that way. But everybody grieves differently. Maybe she's in shock. Can't that give you a sort of absent-minded demeanor?"

"I think that's generous. I was going to say she might be on valium or something. Everyone is telling us how Zoey isn't well off. Even *Zoey* was telling us that when we visited her. You'd think that, even if she was hiding it well, she might be secretly happy that she's finally going to have an influx of cash."

"Unless Zoey wasn't the beneficiary of his will," said Miles slowly.

"If Teddy even *had* a will," said Myrtle. "Younger people often don't."

"Teddy was middle-aged."

Myrtle shrugged. "Like I said. Younger people." She smiled to herself. Miles once again seemed engaged in his sidekick role. This was what she'd been waiting for. "Should we do a recap?"

"Let's do the recap when we get back to your house. I'm not sure I can concentrate on the road and keep the suspects straight at the same time."

Myrtle smiled again. Miles was coming to her *house*. Maybe, after the recap, they could work on puzzles together. Or they could watch *Tomorrow's Promise*. The plot really wasn't nearly as silly as Miles was making out.

Chapter Thirteen

When they walked into Myrtle's living room, Myrtle hurried to get milk and cookies. "Since we didn't have any refreshments at the reception, a little snack might be in order."

Miles seemed amenable to eating store-bought chocolate chip cookies. Which reminded Myrtle about the bread. "Have you tried my bread, yet?"

"The bread?" Miles seemed frozen.

"Yes. The bread I brought you. It was a sweet bread, remember? And it wasn't hard like Elaine's loaves. I did a *much* better job with the starter than she did."

Miles carefully said, "I was saving it for later." Then, with alacrity, "Or I could run by and bring it over now. Bread is good to share with friends."

"No, no. That bread was for you. I'm not going to take it away. That's what a gift is all about. Now, let's get down to business." She handed Miles his glass and a napkin laden with cookies, then settled into the armchair across from where he sat on the sofa.

"The suspects," said Miles, nibbling the very edge of a cookie. Myrtle sincerely hoped he wasn't going to suddenly morph into the health-conscious person he sometimes turned into when they'd eat at the diner. It was most annoying.

"Yes. So first, we have Curtis Walsh. He was Teddy's next-door neighbor and rather vexed at having Teddy's business right beside him."

Miles nodded. "Although, to be fair, it is primarily a residential neighborhood. Having large trucks and customers coming and going would be disruptive to anyone."

"True. And Nat, our developer friend, said Curtis had been furious his son had gotten a broken arm and a truck had blocked his driveway so he couldn't take him to the hospital."

Miles made a face. "That would definitely be aggravating. Although perhaps not quite as aggravating as having a development on your own property blocked. Which is what happened to Nat."

"Yes. I'm sorry you weren't there when Wanda and I spoke with Nat Drake. It was an interesting conversation. Naturally, he played it off very coolly, as if it was just something that happened when one was in business. He did admit he'd gone over to Teddy's shop to try to reason with him."

Miles said slowly, "But how would that have made a difference? Hadn't Teddy already reported the presence of the endangered species to the authorities?"

"Apparently not. Nat said this was right before Teddy reported it. Teddy felt strongly about the salamander, from all accounts. Anyway, Nat said that there wasn't really a motive for him to have murdered Teddy."

Miles frowned. "I don't see that at all. It seems as if he had plenty of motive."

"According to Nat, once Teddy reported the salamander's presence in the stream, it was out of his hands. Nat would have had nothing to gain by murdering Teddy."

Miles said, "What if it wasn't a matter of gaining something? What if it was more a matter of getting revenge?"

"That's what I thought. But Nat acted as if he didn't hold any personal animosity against Teddy." Myrtle paused. "Then we have Ollie Spearman, Teddy's former employee at Blossom Serenade. Wanda and I also spoke with him at the garden club meeting."

"How did that go?" Miles focused on eating his cookies. Myrtle was pleased to see they were rapidly disappearing. Maybe the sugar would sweeten his mood a little.

"It was fine. But I had the feeling Ollie was lying through his teeth. I told him I'd return to do a profile on him for the new shop. Now that Teddy is gone, there's a dearth of florists again. And Ollie could use the publicity."

"What was he lying about?" asked Miles.

"In particular? He said he had an amicable parting of the ways with Linda. That he'd basically given her his blessing to date Teddy. But that doesn't seem to be the case. Plus, he acts as if he was the one who decided to leave the floral shop. However, everything I've heard contradicts that. I think he must have been fired, then decided to try to save face."

"And kill Teddy for revenge?" asked Miles.

"Maybe. He couldn't have been happy about Teddy's treatment of him. After all, he thinks of himself as a genuine talent. Tippy was giving him quite an enthusiastic introduction at the garden club meeting. Maybe his ego took a real beating. Teddy thought Ollie's arrangements were too avant-garde for Bradley. That might have hurt his feelings."

"Who else do we have for suspects?" asked Miles slowly. Then he said, "Oh. Zoey."

"Yes. Zoey is something of a mess, isn't she? The poor thing can't seem to pull herself together to save her life. She's her own worst enemy. Unless she thought *Teddy* was her own worst enemy. From what Linda was saying, Teddy did a lot to help out Zoey. Maybe Zoey, even though she was on the receiving end of that help, became resentful. She was likely jealous Teddy was doing so well and that their aunt made him the beneficiary of her will."

Miles nodded. "That would be enough to make anyone upset."

"It sounds like Zoey doesn't make the best financial decisions. But that might have leaked into her personal life, too. She apparently had a terrible marriage and an equally-awful divorce. So that's Zoey. Last, but not least, is Linda, whom we spoke with at the reception. What did you make of Linda?"

Miles said, "It seems odd that she acted as if she and Teddy were still an item. You said they'd definitely split up?"

"That's what I heard from both Ollie and Zoey. They said Teddy was the one who dumped Linda. It would be nice if I could ask Red about it, to find out if Linda told them the truth or made it seem as if she was still dating Teddy." Myrtle brightened. "I could call Lieutenant Perkins. I haven't had the opportunity to speak with him."

Miles shifted uncomfortably. "That's probably not a great idea. He's got to be busy right now, handling the murder investigation."

"Pish. Perkins loves speaking with me. It'll only take a minute, and I might get some useful information. Red never gives me any information unless it's by accident."

Miles said, "Can you at least have it be a quid pro quo type of thing? Offer Perkins information in exchange?"

"An excellent idea, Miles. What should I present him with? A tidbit on Curtis, perhaps? Nat gave that information to me about Curtis blowing up at Teddy, and perhaps Perkins and Red don't know about it yet." Myrtle pulled out her phone and punched in a phone number.

"Mrs. Clover?" asked Perkins's courteous voice. "How are you doing?"

"I'm doing just fine, Perkins. How are things with you? And how's your dear mama?"

Perkins said, "She's doing all right, ma'am, thanks."

Myrtle said, "I don't want to keep you because I know how busy you are. I wanted to let you know that I came across a nugget of information that I wasn't sure got passed along to you."

"Got it. Thank you. I've got my notebook out."

Myrtle very much enjoyed being the one to impart information. She liked it so much that she was in danger of forgetting the underlying reason for her phone call. "I was speaking with Nat Drake, the developer. He did tell me he'd informed the police that he'd been in Teddy's shop days before Teddy's death. But what he might not have passed along is that while he was in the Blossom Serenade, Curtis Walsh came by. Apparently, Curtis was mad as a wet hen."

"Was he? What happened between Curtis and Nat?"

"Hmm? Oh nothing happened between Curtis and Nat. No, Curtis was angry at Teddy. Curtis's little boy had fallen from the climbing wall in their yard and broken his arm. Curtis hadn't been able to leave his driveway to drive him to the hospital because a delivery truck was blocking his exit."

Perkins said, "I see. That must have been upsetting for Curtis Walsh."

"It was. Curtis seems to have had a history of getting irritated with Teddy. Teddy got rid of a bunch of invasive plants and shrubs that had afforded Curtis some privacy. He also said it was noisy at the floral shop with the trucks coming and going and customers arriving and leaving. He sounded quite vexed about it all."

Perkins said, "Well, I appreciate your coming forward to let me know. I'll be sure to check this out."

Myrtle said sweetly, "Oh, it was my pleasure. There was something else I wanted to ask, though." She paused. Actually, there was more she wanted to ask, aside from whether Linda had disclosed Teddy's breakup with her. She decided to start with the information Red didn't provide her with. "I was curious whether there was any physical evidence recovered at the scene of Teddy's death."

Perkins said, "I can confirm there was. Physical evidence that wasn't a match for anyone in our database. But it will be helpful when we're needing to make our case in court against whoever the defendant ends up being."

"Excellent," said Myrtle. "And I had another quick question for you. I've heard all sorts of things about Linda, Ollie, and Teddy. It's a very tangled love triangle. I was wondering Linda Lambert informed you that her relationship with Teddy had ended."

"Not from Ms. Lambert herself. But from the information we gathered from others, it appears they were *not* dating at the time of the murder."

"Not dating. Got it. Thanks, Perkins."

Perkins said, "Please be careful, Mrs. Clover."

"Yes, I know how irritated Red gets about my investigating."

Perkins said gently, "I think it's more that he's *worried* about your investigating. He doesn't want anything to happen to you."

This startled Myrtle into a momentary silence. "Is that what he's said to you?"

"He hasn't had to. It's very obvious. And I'm worried about you, too. It would be a terrible loss for all of us if something was to happen to you."

Myrtle said, "That's very kind of you, Perkins. But please don't worry. Everything is under control. I'll talk with you soon." And she hung up.

"Everything is under control?" asked Miles wryly. "That seems unlikely."

"Well, it soon will be, even if it's not right now. Were you able to hear what Perkins said to me? I know these cell phones blast their volume."

Miles said, "I think I got the gist of it, anyway. There's physical evidence from the crime scene, and Teddy and Linda had indeed broken up prior to the murder, although Linda hadn't admitted that to the authorities."

"That's right. So now we know." Myrtle turned on the TV. "*Tomorrow's Promise*? I could stick in some microwave popcorn."

Miles didn't seem very enthusiastic. "I might head home for a quick nap."

"The plot is thickening on the show, you know. Flaubert is engaging in an attempted coup."

Miles frowned. "A coup in France?"

"No, somewhere in South America."

Miles said, "Isn't Flaubert French?"

Myrtle said impatiently, "His nationality has nothing to do with it."

"If he's involved in a coup, I'd say it's very important."

Myrtle bit her tongue, literally, before it ran away with her. She was trying to coax Miles into staying, not run him off by squabbling over plot points in the soap opera. "Does popcorn and the show sound good?

Miles stood up. "Maybe I'll catch it with you next time."

"Okay." Myrtle watched as he walked out the door, carefully closing it behind him. Then she picked up the phone again and called Wanda.

"Thought yew might be callin'," drawled Wanda.

"Did you? Good. That means I don't have to try to explain what just transpired with Miles. If, in fact, I *could* explain it, which seems unlikely."

"Think I gotta answer for ya."

Myrtle perked up. "An answer? You mean a reason Miles is acting so out of character? So . . . reserved?"

Wanda said, "The Sight flashed on me early today. Valentine's Day wuz a sad anniversary."

"Sad? You mean Miles has been *sad* all this time? I've been thinking he was ridiculously moody. What on earth could he be sad about?"

Wanda said gruffly, "Asked his wife to marry 'im on Valentine's Day."

"Shouldn't that be a happy memory and not a sad one?"

"Lost 'er on Valentine's Day, too."

"Oh," said Myrtle. She frowned. "So Miles has been dwelling on Maeve's death. Gracious. Her death was a long time ago, though, wasn't it? It's hardly something that should be fresh in his mind. And why hasn't he been brooding during other Valentine's Days?"

"Dunno."

Myrtle said, "I'll find out. Thanks for letting me know, Wanda. I'll talk with you later."

Chapter Fourteen

After Myrtle hung up, she headed for her desk where her computer sat. There she pulled up the obituary for Maeve Bradford of Atlanta, Georgia. She saw a picture of a pleasant, sensible-looking woman smiling. The obituary was glowing, mentioning Maeve's background as a mathematician and engineer, as well as a loving mother. And it said she'd died ten years ago on Valentine's Day.

"A milestone," murmured Myrtle. It all made a bit more sense now. Although it did seem somewhat maudlin of Miles to dwell on it.

While Myrtle was on the computer, she looked up all sorts of things. First up was Nat Drake, the friendly local developer. He was clearly someone who was out and about a lot, networking. In one picture, Nat was showing off his perfect teeth while grasping an oversized pair of scissors and cutting a ribbon for a new development. In another, Nat was in a tuxedo, chatting with members of the Bradley town council. In yet another, he was on the golf green, mid-swing, with men who were likely business associates. The photos went on and on: open houses, community meetings, fundraising dinners, holiday parties, and charity runs. It made Myrtle wonder how he could find time to fit in actual work. Aside from the discovery that Nat was quite the social butterfly, Myrtle couldn't find anything else particularly interesting about the man.

Out of curiosity, she pulled up Zoey Hartfield to see what she could find. Her LinkedIn profile was exceedingly out of date, but listed her as a retail associate a number of years ago. She'd also posted some time ago on an online community bulletin board, offering to do odd jobs like dog walking and babysitting. Myrtle was also quickly able to locate online court documents related to Zoey's acrimonious divorce. There was a divorce decree that went into the division of assets that seemed to favor Zoey's ex-husband. Myrtle felt herself growing sleepy. She switched over to Zoey's social media and ran into quite a few rants on the ex-husband, old employers who'd crossed her, and life in general. It seemed Zoey was not particularly pleased with her life.

Myrtle then looked up the lovely Linda Lambert. It seemed everyone spent a good deal of their lives on social media. But then, to be fair, Linda had a business to run. She had an elaborate website that showcased her professional portfolio. There were branding and menu designs for various restaurants, logo and packaging designs for trendy boutiques, fundraising posters and social media graphics for nonprofits, and class schedules and social media content for fitness studios. It went on and on. It appeared Linda made a decent living off her graphic design.

Curtis Walsh didn't have much of a presence online at all. There was a mention of him in a church bulletin as the father of a child being baptized. He was also mentioned as a surviving son in his father's obituary. Myrtle supposed, as a contractor, that he wouldn't need to have a web presence. It was likely a word-of-mouth thing, since Curtis had clearly been in the line of work for a while.

Then Myrtle looked up Ollie Spearman and found what looked like a brand-new website for his brand-new business. Some pages on the website had "coming soon" on them. Myrtle wondered if Linda had helped with the web design, or whether Ollie had been too angry with Linda to contact her for help. She remembered how Linda had speedily left Teddy's memorial when Ollie seemed to look in her direction. Ollie's website, although incomplete, was already very appealing. The homepage featured beautiful photos of floral arrangements and a welcome message. The services page encouraged visitors to inquire about weddings, event decorations, funerals, and custom bouquets.

But where Myrtle really found activity was on Ollie's social media. She tut-tutted. Really, anyone in the business world should realize that you didn't put things on social media unless you wanted the entire world to see them. Ollie appeared to use social media to gripe about politics and people he knew. She raised her eyebrows when she saw an angry post on Teddy's page. "You'll be sorry," it said. Well, well.

Tiring of the computer, Myrtle settled back into her armchair in the living room. She didn't want to watch *Tomorrow's Promise* without Miles there. It wasn't as much fun. When they watched it together, they got to snipe at the characters, exclaim over the plots, and try to guess what might happen next. Myrtle decided to see what might be on. It turned out to be a documentary on a rock band Myrtle had never heard of. She set the volume low and proceeded to drift in and out of a nap while she watched the band's swift rise in popularity and its chaotic fall from grace.

Sometime later, Myrtle woke with a start. "For heaven's sake," she muttered. It was two o'clock in the morning. She hadn't even eaten supper. Myrtle hoisted herself out of her chair, stretched, and headed for the kitchen to see what she might scrounge up to eat.

The pantry was looking rather bare. The fridge was equally unimpressive after a couple of days of hearty eating. Myrtle made a face. Eggs, olives, coconut milk. She wondered why she even had coconut milk in the fridge at all. None of it made any sense. What would scrambled eggs taste like if they were scrambled with coconut milk? She wasn't sure she wanted to embark on a culinary adventure at this time of the night. She settled for eggs with no milk.

Myrtle realized she had laundry to fold, a task she hoped might make her sleepy. But after folding everything, she felt even peppier than she had before. By this point, she decided she must be up for the day, having gotten enough sleep after her ill-gotten nap the day before. She set about doing other light housework, showering, and dressing. By the time she'd done all that, the newspaper had arrived, and she could work on the crossword.

There was a tap at her door at five-thirty. Myrtle smiled as she walked over to the door. It must be Miles. However, just to be sure, she peeked out to make sure Erma wasn't standing on her doorstep with some sort of grotesque medical emergency.

Fortunately, it was indeed Miles there. She gestured him in. "Coffee?"

Miles nodded. He looked at his friend, frowning. "Wow. You're completely ready for the day."

"You are too."

"Yes, but just in the last forty-five minutes. You have the appearance of someone who has been up most of the night. And are you highly caffeinated or just lively?"

Myrtle said, "Just lively. The longer I've been up, the zippier I've been. Who knows what I'll be like by the end of the day."

Miles fervently hoped he wouldn't be around to witness a hyperactive Myrtle.

Miles followed Myrtle into the kitchen and doctored the cup of coffee she brought him.

"I'd offer you some food, but I don't seem to have any," said Myrtle with a shrug. "Grocery shopping is clearly on my list of things to do today."

"How about if we go to the diner in a little while?" asked Miles.

Myrtle quirked an eyebrow. "You seem to have a tough time finding a non-greasy, low-cholesterol breakfast option there."

"Well, there's always oatmeal. And I could probably handle a biscuit, although the amount of butter they cook them in is pretty decadent," said Miles.

"Okay. We'll head over there right when they open. We'll be early birds."

In the meantime, Myrtle gave Miles the sudoku to solve while she pulled out her crossword puzzle book and worked on the next puzzle in it.

After a while, they set out in Miles's car for the diner. It was foggy out, and Miles was peering cautiously out the windshield as he navigated down the dark streets. Suddenly, the darkness was pierced by red and blue lights and the din of sirens.

Miles pulled to the side of the road to let the emergency vehicles pass them. Afterwards, Myrtle said, "Let's follow them, Miles."

"We're not ambulance chasers, are we?"

"I'm less interested in the ambulance than the police car," said Myrtle.

"Still. We don't want to be lookey-loos."

"No, we don't. But this may not be a medical emergency or a fire. It very well might be a murder. Let's find out," said Myrtle.

Miles heaved a long-suffering sigh and pushed gently on the accelerator, edging back onto the road. At a steady pace, he followed the vehicles, many, many car lengths behind. He turned down a road, passing another vehicle coming out quickly from the area.

The emergency vehicles were parked at a new home construction site. The frame of the house was up, with wooden beams and studs exposed. Some walls were covered with plywood, while others were still open. There were scattered tools and materials on the grounds: hammers, saws, drills, piles of lumber, bags of cement, and stacks of bricks.

"What are they doing here?" asked Myrtle, face up against the passenger window. Impatiently, she put the window down and stuck her head out into the chilly air. "This is the middle of nowhere."

"It appears someone wanted to build a house in the middle of nowhere," said Miles.

"Nothing's on fire. No one lives here . . . not legitimately, anyway. And it seems too early in the day for construction to be taking place. The sun hasn't even risen yet. We're still in that weird twilight. We should hop out and investigate."

"We should not hop out," said Miles firmly. "There's something going on there. Something big," he added as more emergency vehicles arrived on the scene.

Myrtle was still peering into the darkness. "That looks like Hank."

"What looks like Hank?"

Myrtle said, "That burly man over there. He was one of my students. A good one, at that." She called out to him, and the man lumbered over. He frowned until he reached the sedan and saw Myrtle in the passenger seat.

"Why, Miss Myrtle!" he exclaimed. "How are you doing?"

"Oh, just fine, Hank. My friend Miles and I were out early this morning and wanted to find out what was going on when we spotted the firetruck and police cars. Do you know what happened?"

Hank nodded somberly. "Afraid I do. I listen to the police radio. I find out all kinds of stuff that way. When I heard the cops were heading to the construction site, I figured I better check on things. I work on this site, you know. Anyway, it's Curtis Walsh. I don't know if you know him, but he's dead."

Chapter Fifteen

"Curtis is dead?" Myrtle and Miles exchanged a glance. Myrtle continued, "I'm so sorry to hear that. What happened? Was it some sort of medical emergency? Heart attack? Isn't it awfully early to be on a job site?"

Hank nodded. "Too early, for sure. And from what the cops were saying, it sure sounds like murder, Miss M. I can't hardly believe it. Curtis was a great guy."

"You didn't happen to see poor Curtis there, did you? Or were you kept back by the police."

Hank said, "The cops hadn't set up their perimeter then, and I didn't know it was a crime scene. I could see him sprawled out on the foundation. Foundation's just half-finished. A framing hammer was beside him. Looked like somebody had hit him upside the head with it."

Myrtle shook her head. "Horrors. I don't know what a framing hammer is. Is it like a regular hammer?"

"Yes ma'am, but a bit heavier. Carpenters use them." He sighed. "I really liked Curtis, too. Can't believe this happened to him."

"Has anything seemed off with Curtis lately? Has he seemed worried? Has something been on his mind, do you think?" asked Myrtle.

Hank started off saying no, then stopped and thought for a few moments. "You know, I was going to say no, but he hasn't exactly been himself lately. Curtis has been real absent-minded, and that wasn't like him. He was making mistakes on the site. I was starting to get worried he was going to be fired."

"What kinds of mistakes?" asked Miles.

"Miles was a developer," said Myrtle, shrugging.

"An engineer," Miles said through gritted teeth.

Hank said, "Well sir, they were big mistakes and small ones. On the smaller side, he'd cut lumber too short. Wasted our materials. He forgot to put on his safety gear and set up safety barriers. I chalked that stuff up to Curtis being tired. He's a dad, you know, and dads don't get a lot of sleep sometimes."

"But then there was a bigger mistake?" asked Myrtle.

"Yep. Curtis ignored the blueprints and deviated from the architectural plans. Created all kinds of chaos and errors. I've never seen him do something like that before," said Hank.

"Any idea what was on his mind?"

Hank shook his head. "I sat down to talk with him about it after the blueprint thing happened. But he didn't tell me what was on his mind. Just that he hadn't been concentrating enough." Hank paused. "He did say he was about to come into a windfall, though."

"A windfall?" chorused Myrtle and Miles.

"That's right. Didn't say what it was. I reckoned he was coming into some family money or something. And that maybe he was planning what to do with it and that was what was making him so distracted." Hank shrugged helplessly. "But now this has happened. Makes you wonder, don't it? Doesn't it?" He quickly corrected himself, looking over at his old English teacher.

"It does," said Myrtle, gazing toward the police cars.

Hank looked at his watch. "Reckon I should head back home and get ready to come back on the job."

"Not on *this* job, surely. It's a crime scene."

Hank nodded. "Yeah, I've got another job I'm juggling, too. Those folks are going to get me helping out a day early."

"Hank, one other thing. Do you know how the police were aware of Curtis's death? Was there someone else who reported it?"

"I talked to one of Red's deputies for a minute. He said a neighbor heard somebody yelling over here and called the cops." Hank shook his head. "It's an awful thing, ain't . . . isn't it? Good seeing you, Miss M. Nice meeting you, sir." With that, Hank headed to a white pickup truck.

Miles said, "He seems like a nice guy."

"Nicer than Curtis, for sure. I get the feeling that Curtis must have been doing some blackmailing."

Miles slowly started driving back the way they'd come in. "The mention of the windfall, I'm guessing?"

"Right. And the fact Curtis lived directly next to the floral shop. He'd have been able to see someone there who wasn't supposed to be there. If there had been anything suspicious, he could have tried to capitalize on it."

Miles said, "You think that's why Curtis was at a deserted construction site before daybreak? He was meeting someone for a payoff?"

"I don't think he was there to work," said Myrtle tartly. "He wouldn't have even been able to see what he was doing." She frowned. "Where are we going?"

"Home."

Myrtle was displeased by this. "But we were hungry. I had no food at my house, remember? We were heading for the diner."

"But then fate intervened. I wonder if maybe we should just go to my house and have cheese on saltine crackers."

"Miles, what on earth is going on with you?" demanded Myrtle. "You've been behaving so oddly lately. Now you're talking about fate."

"Wanda always talks about fate and people eat it up," noted Miles.

"Yes, but she's a psychic." Myrtle paused. "This all has to do with Maeve, doesn't it?"

Miles looked stoically out the windshield. "What makes you think that?"

"Our aforementioned psychic friend. Plus, I did a bit of research, which indicated her death took place on Valentine's Day. And this happens to be a milestone year, doesn't it?"

Miles sighed, looking tired. "Yes, it is." He glanced quickly across at her. "You're not upset about Stanley? Or at least missing him?"

"My husband Stanley? He died over four decades ago, Miles. It's ancient history. I think about him from time to time of course." In fact, Myrtle rarely thought about Stanley. It was all a lifetime ago and seemed very fuzzy and ethereal.

"I suppose I think about Maeve more frequently." Miles tightened his grip on the steering wheel.

"Isn't that rather maudlin, though? Aren't you dwelling on something that makes you unhappy?"

Miles shook his head. "Maeve never made me unhappy."

"Yes, but her absence clearly is."

Miles pulled into Myrtle's driveway. "I probably just need some time alone to think." His voice was slightly cool. Myrtle clearly hadn't understood the way he'd hoped she would.

Myrtle sighed as she walked back up her driveway, giving Miles a wave. Apparently, he wasn't inviting her in for cheese and saltine crackers after all. She'd hoped Miles was rid of the mopes. Maybe he'd shake it off soon. In the meantime, she had an item of business she needed to attend to.

Myrtle called Sloan to inform him about the new story she needed to write. "I'm sending over the story on poor Curtis Walsh's demise now," said Myrtle.

Sloan sounded alarmed. "Curtis Walsh? What happened?"

"What often seems to happen in Bradley. He was murdered." Myrtle paused. "It's a big story, of course. Is Imogen on-board to copyedit?"

Myrtle knew her story wouldn't need to be copyedited at all. It was completely free of errors. But she wanted to know if her previous efforts to dissuade Imogen had been successful. Had Imogen quit her position as copyeditor?

To her dismay, Sloan said, "Yes ma'am, she's on it. Miz Winthrop does a great job." He quickly realized his mistake, stammering, "Not as great as you do, of course. But you've already got enough on your plate."

Myrtle was quite displeased to hear her endeavor had been in vain. Perhaps she should try again to point out Imogen's deficiencies to Sloan. "You're not having any issues with her outdated grammar rules? I'd imagined they might conflict with modern journalism style guides."

This was news to Sloan. "Outdated rules? In what way?"

"Oh, I'm sure it will all be just fine. It just might make the *Bugle* sound a bit stilted. Charmingly archaic."

Sloan apparently didn't like the idea of the newspaper sounding antiquated. "Hm. Okay. How outdated are we talking?"

"Just minor things, really. Imogen will never split an infinitive. She'll insist on 'whom' in objective cases. There will be absolutely no conjunctions at the start of a sentence. And, naturally, she'll insist on 'shall' for first-person future tense."

There was silence on the other side of the line. "O-kay," said Sloan slowly.

"My only concern is that the paper might seem stuffy and out of touch with modern readers. It could mean the newspaper's content is less engaging." Myrtle was quite pleased with her word choice. 'Engagement' was Sloan's favorite buzzword.

"Engagement," muttered Sloan under his breath.

Not wanting to oversell things, Myrtle said, "Anyway, I'm sure the paper will be well edited. Now I really must go. Things to do, people to see."

"Bye, Miss Myrtle."

With any luck, Sloan would now have food for thought.

A FEW MINUTES LATER, Myrtle was calling Wanda. She told her about Miles, about his rather irritating devotion to Maeve, and about his plan to have alone time to think.

"Reckon he jest needs time," said Wanda. "Want me to drive ya to see Ollie?"

"How did you know I was going to talk with Ollie? Never mind . . . psychic. Speaking of being a psychic, I was wondering how things were going with your wealthy patron. Clarissa?"

"Cassandra," drawled Wanda.

"That's right. How are things going with her?"

"Okay, I guess. But I don't always tell her nice stuff. I think she wants nice stuff."

Myrtle said, "Don't we all? What are the kinds of things Cassandra wants insight on? She's British, isn't she?"

"Lady Cassandra," said Wanda, her voice wry.

"Ah. Yes."

Wanda said, "She wants to know should she invest in a tech startup. If she should call her sister, who she ain't seen fer years. What her dreams mean. If she'll find true love."

"Will she? Find true love?"

Wanda said sadly, "Don't look like it." She paused. "Want me to drive over now?"

It would take a while for Wanda to reach Myrtle, based on her low rate of speed and the distance she must cover. Myrtle agreed she should set out as soon as possible. "I'll pay for your gas," said Myrtle.

Wanda said, "Yew ain't gotta do that. Yew don't git paid fer weeks."

"Yes, but that's really fine."

"And you ain't got any food in th' house."

"Well, that's true," admitted Myrtle. "I suppose I should contribute gas money when my retirement pay shows up in my account."

"Only if yew think about it. Be there in a jiffy."

Chapter Sixteen

It hadn't been a jiffy, of course, but Wanda had arrived as soon as she could. Myrtle climbed into her car, and they set off for Ollie's. Myrtle had given him a heads-up that she was coming over to take pictures and talk with him for the feature article. She wanted to make sure Ollie wasn't attending church, since it was Sunday morning, after all. As expected, he'd sounded delighted and assured her he was skipping church that morning. She wondered if Ollie had heard about Curtis's untimely demise. He must have had interactions with Curtis, too, since he'd worked right next-door to him.

They pulled up into Ollie's house, which was an old Craftsman-style home in an older neighborhood. The yard was full of all sorts of shrubs and decorative trees. Myrtle was sure it must be gorgeous in the springtime. Wanda carefully parked in the driveway. "Figure I'm gonna keep my mouth shut in there."

"You can pretend to be the photographer, if it makes you feel more involved."

Wanda shook her head. "Nope. Not used to phones."

"All right then. Don't feel you have to be quiet, though. Especially if you think of a good question to ask Ollie."

They walked down the cobblestone walkway to Ollie's front door. Ollie answered the door immediately, beaming at them.

"Good morning, ladies. It's good to see you both."

Myrtle said, "You remember Wanda. She's helping me out by driving me around."

"Not driving anymore, are we?" asked Ollie with a smile.

Myrtle greatly disliked when someone used pronouns that way. But she bared her teeth in a smile. "We're not, no."

Ollie ushered them inside a nice, if modestly decorated home that was dotted with houseplants. There was lots of antique furniture.

Ollie saw Myrtle glancing at the furniture. "Some old family pieces."

"They're very nice."

Ollie gestured to a silk settee. "Please, take a seat."

Myrtle and Wanda sat down. Myrtle took out a stenographic notebook from her large purse. "I'm glad this time worked out for you, Ollie. I'm thinking a feature in the newspaper will provide a nice spotlight for your fledgling business."

"Yes, I think it will. I couldn't be more delighted. The timing is perfect."

Myrtle said, "Before we get started, did you hear about Curtis Walsh?"

Ollie frowned, thinking. "Curtis Walsh. Oh, the guy who lives next door to Blossom Serenade. No, I haven't heard any news. Is he okay?"

"I'm afraid he's been murdered. Early this morning."

Ollie's eyes opened wide. "I can't believe it. What happened?"

"Well, we don't have too much information. But it appears someone murdered him at a worksite before sunrise. Odd, isn't it?"

Ollie nodded, still frowning. "Very odd. What are the police saying?"

"I haven't spoken to Red today." It was actually rather miraculous that Red hadn't spotted Miles's car at the crime scene that morning. She was glad she didn't have to defend her investigating again. It was getting rather tiresome. She added, "Red's usual thing is to go by and speak with everyone he spoke with the first time."

"Meaning Red will come by here?" asked Ollie.

"Correct. If he follows his usual routine."

Ollie sighed. "Well, once again I'm alibi-free. I wish I knew when I needed one so I could plan in advance." He made a face. "Sorry. That must sound very callous. I do feel really bad about Teddy. I didn't know Curtis much at all, except I realized he wasn't happy having Teddy as a next-door neighbor. Or Teddy's business, really."

"You're sure nobody can attest to where you were?" asked Myrtle innocently. "You weren't on a phone call with anyone, taking an order this morning?"

"Not early this morning, no. This was the one day I didn't even take my usual walk around the lake. I'd slept in and then organized my workspace. And I only wish business were brisk enough that I would be getting calls all hours of the day and night. Only my fish were witnesses to my presence here." He gestured to a large aquarium across the room. "I was up at about eight o'clock and then was working on arrangements at home around nine-thirty. That's just a rough estimate. I've been having a tough time figuring out a work routine at home. I'm trying to behave like I'm in an actual office."

Myrtle said, "I'm sure you'll figure it out."

"There's just a lot more distractions at the house than when I worked at Blossom Serenade. There, it was just work-related stuff. Here, I know the dishwasher has stopped, and I should unload it. Or I'll see I need to wipe down a mirror that has fingerprints on it. It's just constant distraction." Ollie glanced over curiously at Wanda again. "You were at the garden club meeting."

Wanda nodded shyly.

"You look so familiar. And your name is familiar, too. Wanda is an unusual name."

Myrtle had the feeling they were in the presence of another fan of Wanda's horoscope column. "Wanda is famous for her horoscopes in the local paper. Perhaps that's what you remember her from."

Ollie nodded, brightening. "That's it! I'm sure you hear this all the time, but could you give me a reading?"

Myrtle was feeling like poor Wanda was getting subjected to pushy customers everywhere they went. She said, "There's a fee, of course. These readings can be exhausting for Wanda, you see. They sap her energy."

Wanda nodded. "But I kin do it."

"Wonderful," said Ollie. He pulled out his wallet and peered inside to check the contents. "I have forty dollars on me. Is that enough?"

It was quite a bit more than Wanda used to get, but not nearly as much as she was receiving from her wealthy Lady Cas sandra. Wanda seemed receptive, though, nodding quietly. Ollie watched her eagerly, clearly anticipating something light and happy . . . new creative endeavors, a romantic connection, travel opportunities, or health and wellness. But Wanda seemed to see something different in his aura and on his palm.

"I'm seein' signs pointin' in different directions," murmured Wanda. She looked up at him. "Yer at a crossroads."

Ollie looked solemn. "True. I'm just embarking on a solo venture. A new business. Can you see what's going to transpire with the shop?"

Wanda was quiet for a few moments, her eyes partially closed as she focused. "I see a ledger. Numbers jumping on its pages. Credits, debits." She shrugged apologetically. "Can't get a lock on it."

Ollie was looking more alarmed as the reading went on. "Does that mean that my business's fortunes will go up and down?"

Wanda shrugged again, looking sorry. "Dunno." She paused again for several moments. Then she added, "I see a broken compass. Needle spinnin' around."

Ollie looked even more panicky. "That doesn't sound good. Does it mean that I'll have issues trying to decide a direction for the new business? Branding it? Figuring out arrangements?"

Wanda looked over at Myrtle for help. Myrtle said crisply, "That's not the way The Sight works. Now, if we're all done with the reading, we have other things to accomplish today."

"Yes, of course," said Ollie. "The feature for the newspaper."

"That's right. Also, though, I'm not only trying to write a story for the paper on Teddy's death, but also Curtis Walsh's.

I need some background for that. Don't worry—you won't be named in the article."

"Oh, okay," said Ollie. "What kinds of things are you looking to know?"

Myrtle said, "Well, I feel you might need to know what people are saying in town about Teddy's murder."

Ollie's brow furrowed. "People are saying I had something to do with it?"

"They haven't come right out and said that." This wasn't true. Zoey had blatantly pointed the finger at him. "But they've said you and Teddy were at odds. That you two didn't have the good work relationship that you've been talking about," said Myrtle.

Ollie said slowly, "I guess the truth is somewhat in-between. I haven't wanted to dwell on the fact that Teddy and I didn't get along as well as I would have liked. Not lately, anyway. It makes me feel guilty, somehow, even though both of us were responsible for the way our friendship was deteriorating. Because it *was* a friendship, not just a work relationship."

"I see," said Myrtle. "So you're wanting to remember the good times with Teddy. He was murdered, and you don't like to recall the way things were left between you."

"I guess." Ollie rubbed his forehead. "Things were just not going well in the month leading up to his death. Linda started dating Teddy. That hurt, no matter what I might have told you. I kept thinking if I said it *didn't* hurt, then I might convince myself that was the case. You know—if you say something often enough, you can wish it into being."

Myrtle nodded. "My understanding is that Teddy ended his relationship with Linda not long before his murder."

"That's right." Ollie paused. "You're not thinking Linda had anything to do with Teddy's death, are you?"

"Gracious, no," said Myrtle genially. "My job isn't to think anything. It's just to report. I like to make sure I get my facts straight, that's all."

Ollie relaxed a little. "I really cared about Linda. I still do. Part of me thinks Linda will come back to me now, especially with Teddy gone."

"But Teddy did break up with Linda?" asked Myrtle.

"That's right. It was very aggravating to me. Putting me through all that, then dumping Linda just a few weeks later? Crazy." Ollie's expression was tight.

Myrtle decided to move on to Curtis. "What can you tell me about Curtis Walsh?"

"Teddy and I tried to be neighborly. We invited Curtis over for coffee. Offered his wife flowers. But he was always shutting us out." Ollie shook his head. "It was discouraging because we didn't need any trouble from the neighbors."

"I'm imagining Teddy took the brunt of the complaints from Curtis?" asked Myrtle. "Considering that he owned the business and lived on the property, too."

"That's right. Teddy told me once that Curtis had banged on the front door late at night. Said our motion detector lights were turning on too often and were streaming into his bedroom so he couldn't sleep." Ollie rolled his eyes. "I mean, he would just come up with anything to give Teddy a hard time. If Curtis had just gotten a set of blackout curtains, that would have solved the whole problem."

"Why were the motion detector lights going off?" asked Myrtle.

"Probably deer. Or maybe because the wind was blowing and it was detecting the tree branches moving. Teddy was determined to keep the motion detectors. He wasn't great at going to the bank every single day and sometimes the cash would accumulate in the office. The lights made him feel a little more secure."

Myrtle nodded. "I guess Teddy was by himself there with cash overnight. Anybody would get worried. So Curtis's issues with Teddy were mostly just petty things, then?"

"Mostly," said Ollie. "But there was something else that really annoyed Curtis. The Blossom Serenade was in an older building that constantly needed repairs. Some repairs were minor, piddling things, but others were bigger. Teddy decided to go with another contractor to fix the place up."

Myrtle raised her eyebrows. "Instead of Curtis. Curtis is an independent contractor, I understand."

"From what I gather, yes. So he'd do some solo jobs for homeowners, and he'd work on bigger jobs as part of a team. Anyway, Curtis was furious about it. I didn't think about that the last time I talked to Red. I should have told him. That would have been a big motive for murder, on top of everything else. Maybe it was the straw that broke the camel's back." Ollie shrugged. "But if Curtis killed Teddy, who murdered Curtis?"

"Last time, you said Nat and Zoey might have murdered Teddy."

"And that still stands. Neither of them were happy with Teddy."

"Don't you think Linda also might have wanted to harm Teddy?" asked Myrtle. "It seems so difficult to imagine that Linda was so laid back about Teddy dumping her like that."

"Linda keeps her emotions very much under control. I can't imagine her killing anyone. I can tell you somebody else who got upset with Teddy. His sister, like I mentioned before."

Myrtle had to agree with him. Zoey certainly seemed to have plenty of motive to murder her brother. She was in terrible financial straits and harbored a grudge because their aunt had left her money to Teddy.

"That woman is a total mess in every way. She makes the absolute worst decisions possible about everything. It's like she's not even an adult, just stuck in some sort of adolescence. All she thinks about is herself. Zoey does whatever *she* wants to do. So she doesn't eat right, doesn't go to the doctor, can't keep a job because she oversleeps. And then she had the gall to be shocked when her aunt gave all her money to Teddy?" Ollie snorted.

"I did hear about that. It sounded like Zoey was very hurt by her aunt's decision."

"Hurt?" said Ollie. "She wasn't hurt—she was furious. She stormed over to Blossom Serenade and started screaming at Teddy that he'd basically stolen money that was rightfully hers. But their aunt knew Zoey was in that arrested adolescence we were talking about. Zoey couldn't be responsible for money because she'd blow it."

Myrtle said, "That was something I wondered about. I visited Zoey at her house after Teddy died to give her a casserole. The outside was a mess, of course, but the inside was totally thread-bare. People have said she blows money, but I can't understand what she's blowing it on because her house doesn't seem to have a lot of stuff in it."

"Alcohol," said Ollie with a shrug.

"Oh. Got it."

"It's another reason she kept getting fired from jobs. Teddy said at first that Zoey would mainly just drink at night. Then she couldn't drag herself out of bed in the morning. So Teddy helped get his sister set up with an evening job as a waitress. But Zoey was drinking on the job sometimes. Any money she got went to rent or booze."

Myrtle said, "That's too bad." She had the feeling that this was about as much information as she could wring out of Ollie Spearman. She brightly said, "Thanks so much. You've really helped fill in the gaps for me and provided some excellent background. Now should we get started on the interview for your feature in the paper?"

Chapter Seventeen

Thirty minutes later, Myrtle and Wanda headed out of Ollie's house. Myrtle said, "Would you like me to drive us back? I know how these spur-of-the-moment readings wear you out. I'm sorry Ollie put you through that."

Wanda shook her head. "I'm okay." She bobbed her head toward the street. "Reckon you'll want to talk to her, anyway."

Myrtle followed her gaze to a powder-blue Volvo wagon with a taped-up window and a mismatched door. The car appeared to be from the early 1990s. The exterior betrayed its age, with rust spots and faded paint. Myrtle recognized it immediately. "That's Zoey's car."

Zoey didn't appear to be getting out of the Volvo, so Myrtle walked up to the passenger window and knocked gently. Zoey jumped, then rolled the window down.

"Sorry, I didn't mean to scare you," said Myrtle.

"It's okay," said Zoey. "I was just lost in my head." She colored a little. "I had Teddy and Ollie on my brain. I thought maybe I'd run by and see Ollie."

Wanda was giving Zoey a piercing look. Myrtle had the feeling that Wanda could see through her lies. What was Zoey really doing here? Was she going to ask Ollie for money in Teddy's stead? After all, it should take a while for Teddy's estate to go through probate, even if he'd had a will. And even if he'd left anything to Zoey at all.

Myrtle said, "Have you seen Red this morning? I was just wondering if maybe he stopped by to see you."

Zoey looked startled. "Red? No. Why would he come talk to me?"

"I'm afraid Curtis Walsh is dead." Myrtle wasn't sure Zoey would pick up on who that even was. She'd seemed so scattered lately, and then Ollie had talked about a dependency on alcohol. But Zoey immediately knew who she was talking about.

"Curtis? Oh, no. No, I didn't know that. What happened to him?" Her thin hand crept up to her throat.

"I'm afraid he was murdered this morning," said Myrtle.

"Oh, no," said Zoey again. She slid down farther into the seat of her car. "What's happening around here?"

"Did you know Curtis well?" asked Myrtle.

"What? No, I never met him. I only heard stories from Teddy. I know the two of them didn't get along well as neighbors." Zoey gasped, her hand clutching her throat tighter. "And he has little kids. This is terrible. Is some crazy person going down their street murdering people?"

It was a rather fanciful way of looking at the two murders especially since the victims were connected. "I don't think that's likely, no," Myrtle said. "I suspect Curtis may have known who Teddy's murderer was. Since he was right next door."

Zoey nodded slowly. "That makes sense. Then the killer had to shut him up before he told anybody. Oh, how awful." She leaned her head back onto the headrest, closing her eyes. Zoey definitely didn't look well.

"Are you all right, Zoey? Do you need medical assistance? Should we get someone to help you?"

"What? No. I'm fine." Zoey opened her eyes, but still looked unwell. "My head's hurting, that's all." Then she gave a short laugh. "Who am I fooling? I'm a total wreck, aren't I?"

Myrtle was worried for a moment that Zoey would suddenly realize who Wanda was and demand a reading, just like the other suspects. Wanda gave Myrtle a wink, apparently knowing what was on her mind. But Zoey was too caught up in her own little world to know or care who Wanda was. Or, perhaps, she didn't particularly want a glimpse into her future. It might not be a cheerful look.

Myrtle realized Zoey seemed to be waiting for an answer to her question. "A wreck? I don't think you're a wreck, no. You've been under a lot of stress lately, haven't you?"

Zoey gave that abrupt laugh again. "I've been under a lot of stress since the day I was born. Nothing has ever gone my way. When I was a kid, I had a hard time focusing in school and stuff. And my parents never gave me the attention they gave Teddy. I didn't learn to read at the right time and was always trying to play catch-up in school."

"Were you dyslexic, perhaps?" asked former schoolteacher Myrtle.

Zoey looked startled at the idea. "Maybe. Who knows? It's not like my mom or dad cared enough to get me tested. Maybe that was the whole reason I was always doing so bad."

Zoey definitely hadn't been Myrtle's star student. But having an issue like dyslexia would certainly explain a lot.

Zoey continued with her litany of woes. "Teddy, on the other hand, was always the pet. Always sitting on my mom's lap with her finger following on the page as she read from the time he was three, on. I guess they didn't want to take a chance that Teddy might end up doing bad in school, too. And college was totally out of the question for me, even community college."

Myrtle strongly doubted this. Even if Zoey had decided on a non-academic track, she would have had plenty of other choices that could have prepared her for a good job. Zoey could have taken business courses or learned programming or become a cosmetologist.

Zoey sighed. "I'm drowning in debt, like I told you before. I can't seem to find work. It's a real problem. And now I'm a suspect in a murder investigation. Great. I'm sure Red is going to think I'm guilty. He acted last time like he thought I was."

"I'm sure Red acts that way when he talks to everybody, Zoey. It's his job, right? Can you give him an alibi for early this morning?"

"Early? Like real early?" asked Zoey.

Time was relative. Really early for Myrtle was three-thirty in the morning. Anything later than that was just regular morning. "Yes. Very early."

Zoey said, "I went to grab coffee at McDonald's because I was out of it at home."

It was plausible. Zoey seemed to be the kind of person who would forget an important purchase like coffee until it was too late.

"Do you think they'd recognize you there? That someone there could give you an alibi?"

Zoey nodded. "Sure. It's always McKenzie working there that early."

"You must be an early bird if you know the staff so well."

Zoey laughed that mirthless laugh again. "Nope. I'm a night owl. It's just that sometimes I haven't gone to bed yet when it's that early."

"Got it." Myrtle gave her a thoughtful look. "When I talked to you last time, you were saying Ollie Spearman was probably the most likely person to have harmed Teddy. Do you still feel that way?"

"Do I? Of course I do. I can't imagine why the cops haven't picked him up yet. Don't they care about Teddy's death at all? And justice?"

Zoey's gaze shifted away, and Myrtle got the impression that Zoey cared little about those things. She simply didn't want to be a suspect herself.

Myrtle said, "Well, I hope things start looking up for you soon, Zoey. I'm very sorry it's all been so hard on you lately. I hope it's not too nosy of me to ask if Teddy had a will."

Zoey slumped even further in her seat. Any more and she'd be looking up at the steering wheel. "Yes, he had a will. But no, he didn't provide for me in it." A determined look crossed her features. "I'm going to get a lawyer and talk to him about it. It's just not fair. Teddy must not have been thinking straight when he wrote that will."

It sounded to Myrtle as if Teddy had been making a smart decision. But it was definitely tough on Zoey. "I'm sorry," Myrtle said again. "I'll keep an ear out and let you know if I hear any-thing about jobs that might be available. I'll see you later."

With that, she and Wanda climbed into Wanda's car.

"I wonder what Zoey's doing in front of Ollie's house," said Myrtle, watching as Zoey stayed there.

Wanda said, "Ain't gettin' no insight on that."

"Maybe she's going to ask Ollie for a job. Although he'd know too much about Zoey to offer her one." Myrtle sighed. "She was right when she said she was a mess. Do you mind if we run by McDonald's? I can treat us to a coffee or something. I suppose it's still early enough for McKenzie to be there."

"Sure," said Wanda, aiming the car in that direction. "Yew wanna check her alibi."

"Yes. Although I have the feeling she doesn't actually have one. None of the suspects do."

They pulled up in the drive-through, Wanda carefully navi-gating her car. A laconic voice welcomed them to McDonald's. Myrtle ordered them both coffees. When they drove around, they saw a young woman with McKenzie on her nametag. She took Myrtle's money from Wanda, and Myrtle leaned over from the passenger side and sweetly asked, "Do you happen to know if a woman named Zoey was in here this morning, getting cof-fee?"

McKenzie gave her a puzzled look, then registered Myrtle's age. Likely figuring it was simply a peculiarity of her advanced years, she said, "I haven't seen her for at least a week."

"Not this morning?"

"Not this morning."

"Did you perhaps take a break from the window at some point? Work the front counter? Take a smoke break?" suggested Myrtle.

McKenzie glowered at her. "I took no breaks. I've been at working this window straight through the morning. Have a nice day." And the drive-through window closed.

"Well, that's very interesting," said Myrtle as Wanda drove them away. "It sounds like Zoey made up her alibi. I can't say I'm completely shocked. Sadly, it doesn't necessarily indicate her guilt. It might just mean she doesn't want to be a suspect, so her life doesn't become even more derailed than it is right now."

"Mebbe," agreed Wanda.

"It's very aggravating that Miles didn't take me to the diner. I was wanting to go there."

Wanda said, "I kin take yew."

"No, thanks. The problem with going now is that it will be totally crowded. No, I'll wait and go tomorrow morning. Maybe I can coax Miles to take me." Myrtle looked at Wanda. "You're welcome to come, too."

Wanda shook her head. "Reckon yew and Miles need to work things out."

"That's very true. It seems very unnatural for the two of us not to be spending much time together. I want to get back to the status quo. But I'm not sure Miles is done pining after Maeve." Myrtle sighed. "I don't mean it in a bad way. I suppose I simply don't understand where he's coming from. When I experience bad things, I move forward as soon as possible."

"He's more sensitive," observed Wanda.

"I suppose he is," said Myrtle in surprise. She climbed out of the car and waved cheerfully to Wanda as she drove away. On her way up her driveway, she glared in displeasure at an ugly weed. It was quite large and was partly underneath an even larger gnome, a gnome inexplicably dressed as an astronaut.

"There are no weeds in space," muttered Myrtle. The entire aesthetic was ruined. She took her cane and shoved at the gnome, hoping to expose the rest of the weed. The gnome continued blithely grinning under his helmet. Then she stooped, trying to pull the interloper out from under the gnome that way. But neither the weed nor the gnome would budge.

"Fiddlesticks," snarled Myrtle.

She heard a large engine coming down the street and ignored it, still trying to yank the weed away. The weed was equally determined to stand its ground.

"Miz Myrtle!" hollered a horrified voice.

Myrtle turned, hands still on the offending weed, to see Dusty yelling at her from his truck. She carefully stood up, wiping her hands on her slacks.

"What're you doin'?" he asked her.

"Pulling an intrepid weed, of course. What does it look like I'm doing?" Myrtle was, by this time, thoroughly out of sorts.

"Looks like yer not pullin' a weed at all. It ain't coming up."

Myrtle said in an exasperated tone. "You noticed."

"Wait there." Dusty sounded just as exasperated as she did by now. He pulled the truck into her driveway and turned off the engine. Then he stomped over to her in his disreputable looking boots. "Here." He reached out, grabbed the weed by the throat of the thing, and ripped it out of the soil, upending the astronaut gnome as he did so.

Although Myrtle was pleased to lose the weed, it was extremely annoying that Dusty had succeeded where she had failed. He wasn't that young of a man. And he wasn't very tall—not as tall as Myrtle's own six feet. But he had that tenacious, wiry strength.

"Thank you," muttered Myrtle.

"My pleasure," he said. "I was just driving from another job and couldn't believe my eyes. What if Red found out you was doin' those kinds of shenanigans?"

"He better not find out," said Myrtle fiercely.

"Okay, okay." Dusty carefully set the astronaut gnome back on his feet again. He studied the octogenarian in front of him. "Let's go inside. You need to wash your hands. An' git some water."

Dusty was right, to Myrtle's further aggravation. During her struggle with the weed, her hands had somehow gotten both covered in red clay and grass-stained. She followed him in meekly, watching as he kicked off his filthy boots at the door, and scrubbed her hands clean while he fixed her a large tumbler of ice water.

"Next time, gimme a call," said Dusty. "You about scared the life out of me."

"Sometimes you won't come," Myrtle pointed out. "Sometimes you look for reasons to avoid doing yard work."

"Just tell me you'll do it yourself," said Dusty grimly. "That'll git me to come." He shook his head. "You need to be more careful. Not just here. There's a killer runnin' around."

Myrtle said, "You heard about Curtis Walsh. Did you know him?"

"Sure. I used to do contractin' work."

This stunned Myrtle. Contracting seemed entirely beyond Dusty's capabilities. Or, at least, beyond his drive. It was extremely difficult to motivate Dusty to do anything. He grinned at her, apparently reading her mind. "Yep. Used to do some contracting here n' there."

"Don't you need a special license for that?" asked Myrtle dubiously.

"Yep."

"Did you *have* the license?" asked Myrtle.

"I had the experience," said Dusty with a shrug. "Sometimes, that was good enough."

"Didn't you like the work? What made you decide to do yard work full-time?"

Dusty chuckled. "Contractin' was too much work."

That she could believe. But owning one's own business wasn't a piece of cake, either. Although, Myrtle supposed, it could be if one had limited drive and little work ethic. Dusty and Puddin were quite the pair in that respect.

"What did you make of Curtis?" asked Myrtle.

"Crooked."

"Was he?" asked Myrtle. She wasn't completely surprised by this statement, but she was surprised Dusty knew Curtis well enough to make it.

"Sure was. Saw him takin' cash sometimes, on the side. Under the table. Reckon he wasn't reportin' that. Used unlicensed workers."

"Like you?" asked Myrtle pertly.

"Yep. Not just me, though. And he was too friendly with suppliers. Think he got kickbacks."

Curtis Walsh did seem like a rather unsavory character. If he'd do things like that, maybe he'd blackmail, as she'd been supposing before.

Dusty made a disgusted face, which seemed to show his opinion of Curtis. "I'm guessing you're not surprised he met his fate via murder?" asked Myrtle.

He shrugged. "Not really."

"Hmm. Okay. How about Teddy Hartfield?"

"Dunno him."

Myrtle said, "Teddy ran the local floral shop. Blossom Serenade."

The look on Dusty's face told Myrtle he was not a frequent customer. That he had perhaps never darkened the doors of the establishment. That Puddin might be continuously bouquet-free. "You've never gotten Puddin flowers before?"

Dusty scowled. "Puddin?"

"Your wife, Puddin. How many other Puddins do we know?"

Dusty gave a long-suffering sigh. "Nope." Then he tilted his grizzled head to one side thoughtfully. "Mebbe. From the Piggly-Wiggly."

Myrtle thought this was acceptable. She was starting to feel sorry for the flowerless Puddin, which annoyed her to no end.

Dusty said, "Gotta move on. Stuff to do." He leveled a serious look at Myrtle. "No more weedin'." With that, he climbed into his truck, fired up the engine, and roared off.

Considering the time, she needed to get the article on Curtis Walsh underway. She set about writing. Forty-five minutes later, she had a well-written and proofed article to email to Sloan.

She supposed she should write the feature on Ollie, as well. There was no time like the present for doing things one didn't particularly want to do. She cobbled together a coherent portrait of Ollie Spearman and his business plan, despite the fact that he didn't seem to have one. At least, not a coherent plan. He only knew he wanted to take over Teddy's mantle as the local florist. Myrtle emailed that along to Sloan as well, along with some pictures she'd taken. Sloan thanked her in a response email. Myrtle asked whether Imogen was still on board at the newspaper. Sloan assured her she was.

Myrtle didn't realize Imogen had such perseverance. In other circumstances, Myrtle might consider it an admirable trait. At this point, it was simply irritating. "Stuff and nonsense," muttered Myrtle to herself.

Elaine had dropped by a perfectly dreadful loaf of bread on Valentine's Day, which proved excellent timing. She decided to walk to Imogen's house and deliver the bread. And, perhaps warnings about how terrible it was to work at the newspaper.

After a longer walk than Myrtle had wanted to take that day she pasted a determinedly cheerful smile on her face as she finally knocked on Imogen's door. Unfortunately, it looked like she was baring her teeth. "Imogen!" she sang out as the old woman answered the door. Today, Imogen was sporting a floral dress and a pastel cardigan. A tired expression crossed Imogen's fea tures. "Myrtle." She stared at the loaf of offending bread, a look of dread on her face.

"I've been baking up a storm and wanted to bring you a special loaf." Myrtle proffered it in both hands, her cane dangling from an arm. Imogen looked at it as if it might be a bomb that needed diffusing.

"That's *really* not necessary," said Imogen. She didn't appear to want to usher Myrtle inside.

"How are you liking the newsroom so far?" asked Myrtle in a perky tone. "Isn't it so quirky and wonderful?"

"Quirky?" asked Imogen. "I wouldn't have described it like that."

"No? You must not have gotten acquainted with the coffee machine. I swear the thing is sentient. And prone to violence."

Imogen quirked an eyebrow.

"You'll find out," said Myrtle, a knowing tone in her voice. "It just makes life interesting in the newsroom." She blinked innocently at Imogen. "Won't the team-building exercises be fun?"

"Pardon?"

"The team-building exercises. Heavens, hasn't Sloan told you about them yet? I thought he'd be more on the ball. They're to create a strong team and develop both our individual and group strengths. Sloan tries to make them as fun as he possibly can."

Imogen did not look enthusiastic.

Myrtle warmed to her topic. "Once, he drove us to Charlotte, to the white-water rafting center there. It was terrifying, but exhilarating."

Imogen frowned. "Aren't you a little old to participate in white-water rafting?"

"Certainly not. Even if you fall out of the raft, it's not as if you're hitting concrete. It's water, after all. This time, he's planned a midnight survival challenge in the mountains. It's going to be amazing."

Imogen backed up. "I'm afraid I won't be able to attend that."

"But it's mandatory. You'll have fun once you get there."

Imogen seemed quite determined. "I meant to tell you earlier, Myrtle. I don't think I'm going to accept the position as copyeditor for the *Bugle*."

Myrtle affected a crestfallen expression. "Oh no! Why ever not? I was sooo looking forward to working with you." She was very pleased with her acting ability. Really, she deserved an Oscar for the performance. For *all* the performances.

"It simply doesn't suit. I'm a very quiet woman and fond of my routine. I'm afraid running off to the newsroom to copyedit random stories isn't going to fit in."

Myrtle said sadly, "What a pity. The random stories are actually the most fun, you know. 'Lost Cat Returns Home After Three-Day Adventure.' 'Library's Overdue Book Amnesty Yields Surprising Return: 1952 Copy of *Charlotte's Web*.'"

Imogen was very firm now. "Yes. Well, the paper will have to figure out their copyediting without my help." She paused "I think you should take your bread back. Considering I'm no longer going to be your colleague."

"No, the bread is yours to keep. Would you like me to bring you more whenever I make it next?" Myrtle was enjoying the various expressions flitting across Imogen's features.

Imogen shuddered. "No thank you. Now, I really must go. I have a list of things to tackle this morning. And I need to contact Sloan about the job."

Myrtle walked back down the cobblestone path, a smile on her face.

Chapter Eighteen

Following the visit with Imogen, she did the next thing on her list, since she was being so very productive. She picked up her phone and dialed Miles.

"Hi Myrtle," said Miles. His voice might have been the slightest bit cool.

"Hi there," said Myrtle. "I was thinking that I'd invite you to Bo's Diner tomorrow morning, since our attempt to eat there was foiled earlier. What do you think?"

Now it appeared Miles might be waffling. "I started thinking about my cholesterol. I probably should just stay at home and eat something healthy."

Precisely what Myrtle was afraid of. Miles needed to get out and about and stop fretting. She said, "You were going to get oatmeal, remember? There's nothing very dangerous about oatmeal."

Miles sounded less interested in the oatmeal than he had that morning. "I don't know—maybe I should just have a bowl of bananas and apples, instead."

Myrtle pressed her lips in a thin line before saying. "There's something else that might fit the bill. There's an egg-white omelet. You can fill it with all sorts of revoltingly healthy things."

"I don't remember an egg-white omelet being on the menu," said Miles slowly.

"It's there. I don't know why you've never chosen it before."

It was probably because Miles never spent much time perusing the menu. He'd latch onto the oatmeal and put the laminated document down on the table.

"I suppose we can go tomorrow morning," said Miles, not sounding in the least enthusiastic.

"Wonderful!" said Myrtle. "Our usual time?"

"What time is that?"

"Seven. Let's go at seven," said Myrtle. "See you then." And she hung up the phone.

The next morning was a chilly, blustery one. She donned a heavy cardigan sweater over a thick blouse and put on a pair of thick cotton pants. Myrtle regarded herself in the mirror. Somehow, she seemed to resemble a snowman. She stuck her tongue out at herself.

Miles tapped on the door. Discouragingly, Miles was able to look like a grown-up human and not a snowman at all. He had on a sensible wool overcoat and a tweed hat.

"You look very professional for our breakfast at the diner," noted Myrtle.

"Old work clothes," said Miles.

"Were Atlanta winters cold enough to justify the purchases?"

Miles said, "Sometimes."

They walked into the diner. A waitress immediately smiled and told them to sit where they liked. Myrtle, upon spotting a preppy man with sandy-blond hair, decided she would like to sit with him.

"Where are you going, Myrtle?" asked Miles with alarm.

"That's Nat Drake. The developer Wanda and I spoke with. I think we should join him."

"Let's not," Miles hissed through his teeth.

"I bet he'll love the company."

"*No one* likes company at this hour," said Miles with conviction.

"You can't know that. After all, you and I like company this early."

Miles said, "Because there's something fundamentally wrong with us."

Myrtle could not be swayed and soon was at Nat's table. He was clearly an early bird too, because he was impeccably dressed for work in a tailored navy blazer, a cashmere scarf, and Oxford dress shoes.

A momentary flash of annoyance crossed Nat's features before being replaced with a gracious grin. "Miss Myrtle? How lovely to see you this morning."

"Good to see you, too, Nat. This is my friend Miles."

Miles gave him an apologetic smile.

Nat said, "Good to meet you."

"Might we join you? It's just such a pleasure for us older folks to be around younger ones. We won't disturb you, will we?" asked Myrtle sweetly.

It was clearly an imposition. Nat had a notebook and graph paper on the table and seemed to be looking at notes for the day. He pressed his lips together briefly, then said, "Of course you can."

"Thank you. It makes the day so much better to break up the retirement routine, you know." Myrtle tittered. "Actually, you *wouldn't* know, would you? You're still working. Every day probably looks very different from the last."

Nat said, "Oh, I wouldn't say that. Some of my days are unpredictable, of course. But the majority of them follow a conventional path." He politely asked, "What did the two of you do before retirement?"

Myrtle said, "I was a high school English teacher. Miles was an architect."

"Engineer," said Miles stiffly.

Nat took a bite of what looked like a Greek omelet. After swallowing it down, he said, "Those must have been very interesting careers." He looked at Myrtle. "I believe you've moved into journalism now, haven't you?"

She was pleased Nat had noticed. But then, he apparently read the newspaper since he'd known who Wanda was because of it. "Yes, I have a regular column there and also do some crime reporting."

"I'd imagine you'd be the right person to write about crime. With your son being the police chief and all. He'd be a very useful source."

Myrtle made a small face. "Well, sometimes Red isn't as helpful as I'd like him to be." Although Myrtle was always rather fond of being the topic of conversation, she felt she needed to move the conversation back to Nat. He seemed like a busy man—one who might quickly spring up and leave for a meeting or a phone call as soon as his rapidly disappearing omelet was finished. "Was your father Turpin Drake?"

Nat smiled. "He was indeed. Did you know him?"

"I taught him."

Now Nat seemed genuinely interested in the conversation for the first time. "Did you? What was he like back then? You know he passed on a few years ago."

"Yes, and I was sorry to hear it. But he'd had a good life, hadn't he? Turpin always seemed to be very successful, whenever I read about him in the paper."

Nat nodded. "He was, yes. He was the one who paved the way for me to become a developer. Was he a good student?"

"Sadly, no. At least not in high school English. He was something of a character. He didn't care about English whatsoever."

Nat gave a peal of laughter, his white teeth gleaming. "Oh that's great. I've always felt a little like Dad was perfect with everything he did. It made it tough to follow in his footsteps. Anytime I talk to anybody about Dad, they're always praising him, talking about what a genius he was in business. So it's great to hear he wasn't perfect in everything."

"Far from it," said Myrtle tartly. "There were a couple of times I worried your father was going to have to repeat my class a second time. It kept me up at night." She gave Nat a curious look. "I suppose Turpin's tremendous success probably came at the cost of family time, didn't it?"

They were momentarily interrupted by the chirpy waitress. She took their orders: oatmeal and a dish of fresh berries for Miles, buttermilk pancakes with a side of crispy bacon for Myrtle. Miles had apparently completely forgotten about the egg-white omelet, but Myrtle didn't want to interrupt their conversation with Nat to remind him about it.

The waitress hurried off, and Nat said, "No, Dad wasn't at home a lot when my brother and I were growing up." He gave a short laugh. "When I was a kid, I thought construction sites were where dads lived. He was in a hard hat more often than he was at the dinner table, that's for sure." He shrugged. "But Dad was a great provider. We had a good life. Private schools, vacations, all that stuff. It reminded me that success came at a price. So I've put off having a family until I get farther along in my career. I don't want to be an absentee parent. When it came down to it, all I really wanted was time with my father."

Miles cleared his throat. "It's smart of you to put off parenting right now."

"Thanks. Right now, I'm just reaching for the next rung on the ladder, you know? But that's what Drake men do. That's what Dad was always telling me, anyway. If you want to make it in this world, you can't let anything stand in your way."

"Not even a bunch of salamanders?" asked Myrtle innocently.

Nat snorted. "Yeah, well, maybe salamanders will stand in my way. Do you know, I had plans to relocate those guys to a totally different place. It was going to be pricey, but I was willing to do it. But I wasn't even allowed to do that. Now I've got property I can't do anything with." He shook his head. "I can just picture what my dad's reaction would have been. He'd have been laughing like crazy, a glass of bourbon in his hand. He'd say he couldn't believe a glorified lizard was going to cost me that much money."

Myrtle said, "Thinking about that property and its proximity to Teddy's, reminds me. Did you know Curtis Walsh was murdered?"

Nat polished off his Greek omelet, nodding. "Heard about that yesterday. I didn't know the guy at all, but I was sorry to hear he was dead. Like I said, I only knew about him because he came over to Teddy's shop to yell at him about delivery trucks blocking his driveway. He was definitely not a happy camper. But I guess I'd be the same way if something happened to my kid."

Myrtle and Miles's food arrived. Miles picked at his fresh fruit as Myrtle dug into her pancakes. Nat frowned. "Miss Myrtle, you don't think Red will come by to talk with me again, do you? I really didn't know Curtis Walsh at all. Perhaps you could let him know that. I wouldn't want to waste Red's time by having him go on a wild goose chase."

"Sadly, I don't have any control over Red and haven't for the last thirty years or so. But I'd imagine that either he or someone from the state police will follow up with you. That's probably just standard procedure."

Nat knit his brows. "But I have nothing else to add."

"Then it'll be a pretty short conversation." Myrtle picked up a piece of her bacon. It was perfectly crispy. "Of course, if you have an alibi for yesterday morning, that would probably take you off Red's list."

"I was catching up on paperwork and admin stuff yesterday morning, from the time I got up until the time I left for the office. I often go to work on a Sunday. With no one else at the office, I get completely organized for the week ahead."

"No one at home with you to verify you were there?" asked Myrtle.

"Like I said, I've put off marrying and having a family."

"No household help?" asked Myrtle.

Nat shook his head. "No witnesses at all."

"What a pity." Myrtle quickly ate her bacon.

He sighed, ruffling his blond hair, then smoothing it back down again. "If only Teddy hadn't found out about the salamanders. I mean, I'm all about progress. Nature adapts, right? If it doesn't, it's survival of the fittest."

"And Teddy didn't strike you as being pro-progress?" asked Miles, pushing his glasses up his nose.

"No. He and I clashed on that subject. But it was business . . . nothing personal. When I went over to ask Teddy to drop the topic, it was a completely civilized conversation. Just an exchange of discourse. There was no personal confrontation at all."

"Unlike Curtis's meeting with Teddy," said Miles.

"Correct. I didn't know Curtis, like I said, but I could tell he was volatile. Not that he didn't have just cause to be angry, of course. Not being able to take your child to the hospital would be infuriating."

Myrtle said, "The last time we talked, you thought Curtis might have murdered Teddy."

"That was total speculation," said Nat. "I don't have any evidence one way or the other. And, since Curtis is gone, I'm thinking I must have been wrong. Unless there is another murderer running around."

"Heavens, let's hope not. Red would lose his mind, if that were the case," said Myrtle. She paused and said, "It's funny you don't remember Curtis, aside from that one incident. When I spoke with him, he said he knew you from various job sites."

Nat's eyes narrowed. "Well then, he has a better memory than I do. I guess he's just blending together in my mind with all the other contractors I've worked with." Nat ran a hand through his hair, his expression a mix of frustration and defensiveness. "Look, you have to understand the scale of what I do. I've been in this business for over two decades, and in that time, I've worked on dozens of projects across multiple states. We're talking about hundreds of contractors coming and going over the years."

He leaned back, gesturing vaguely with his hands. "On any given project, I might interact with electricians, plumbers, carpenters, masons, roofers, landscapers - the list goes on. And for each trade, there might be multiple subcontractors, each with their own crews. It's a revolving door of faces and names."

Nat's tone became more matter-of-fact. "Most of these guys I see them for a day or two, maybe a week, and then they're off to the next job. Unless there's a major issue or they're a key player in the project, they just blend into the background. It's not personal, it's just the nature of the business."

He sighed, shaking his head slightly. "So when you ask me about Curtis, I'm not being evasive. I genuinely don't have clear recollection. He could have been on half a dozen of my sites over the years, and unless he did something to really stand out, good or bad, he'd just be another face in the crowd. That's the reality of construction management—you can't form lasting connections with every worker who passes through your sites."

He picked up the check, which the waitress had laid on the table. "Considering the time, I'd better get on with it. Good seeing you two." He walked up to the counter to pay.

Miles looked relieved that the ordeal was over. "I don't think Nat particularly enjoyed having breakfast with us."

"Oh, he was fine. We just talked about the murders, that's all. If he was uncomfortable, maybe there's good reason for it."

"Talking about murder over breakfast might make anyone uncomfortable," Miles pointed out. "Or perhaps affect their digestion."

"I can't imagine why. It's the topic du jour. I'm certain Nat understands that. He's lived in Bradley his entire life. He knows how gossip works here." She watched as Miles pushed around his oatmeal in his bowl. Her own breakfast was a memory now. Myrtle sighed. She had the feeling she still needed to smooth things over with Miles.

Myrtle considered what she should say. She was quite rusty at apologizing, since she did little of it. She didn't have to—she was ordinarily in the right, at least in her point of view. Myrtle started in an offhand way, "I've been thinking about what you said about Maeve. I know you miss her. Stanley and I were completely different from the two of you, and I think that's why I'm not perhaps relating as well as I might. We had a lot less time together than you and Maeve."

Miles looked up from his oatmeal. "You were in your forties when he died, right?"

"Yes. And now I've been forty years without him. I can barely remember what he was like." Myrtle shrugged. "Once he passed, I had to leap into action—there was no time to mourn. I needed to put food on the table for Red. A lot of food, since Red always had an enormous appetite. Fortunately, I'd taught before Red was born, and my teaching certificate was still active. I hopped right into teaching again. But things were different for you."

Miles nodded, looking thoughtful. "It's sort of like what Nat was saying about his father. Nat's dad was spending long hours working, thinking it was most important to provide for them. But all they really wanted was *him*. It took me a while to come to that realization, too."

"But you did come around to it. Your family is clearly crazy about you."

Miles nodded. "But I wasted a lot of time when I could have been spending it with Maeve and Dana."

"Well, you were understandably busy."

"Being an engineer," said Miles, looking carefully to see if there was recognition of this fact.

"Yes, of *course* I know you were an engineer, Miles! What kind of detective would I be if I couldn't remember my own sidekick's occupation?" She frowned at him. "You look disbelieving."

"Only a little."

"A civil engineer should be more civil," said Myrtle with a sniff.

Miles tilted his head to one side. "Do you even know what a civil engineer does?"

"Keeps things courteous and well-mannered, of course! That's what makes you such a good sidekick. You're so handy when interviewing suspects."

Miles said, "Sometimes you're not very civil, yourself. Particularly when it comes to offering meals to the bereaved."

Myrtle scowled at him. "That wouldn't be a jab at my cooking, would it?"

"It would be uncivil to answer that honestly."

Miles eventually finished playing with his oatmeal. "Time to go?" he asked.

Myrtle nodded. She noticed with relief that his mood seemed lighter. He paid the bill for both of them, and they left the diner.

"Back to your house for more coffee and puzzles?" asked Miles.

Myrtle was about to answer when something caught her eye across the street. "Pull over."

"What?"

Myrtle said impatiently, "Linda Lambert is over there. At the coffee shop . . . see her through the window? I should talk to her."

Miles looked loath to impose himself on yet another unsuspecting person that morning. "Myrtle, I think it's better if we just head back to your house. Leave the poor woman alone. It looks like she's working. She has her laptop out. Speak with her another time."

"The problem is that it's hard *finding* another time with someone like Linda. She works from home. I don't exactly have need for graphic design materials, so I don't have a good excuse to visit her." Myrtle gestured across the street. "Just park right in front of the coffee shop. You don't have to join me if you don't want to."

Miles frowned. "Then I'll be sitting in my car watching the two of you and looking creepy."

"Then take a walk! You always talk about needing more exercise."

"I'm quite sure I don't," said Miles in a firm voice. "And it's rather chilly outside this morning."

"You're wearing a wool coat. And a tweed hat. You look very dapper. Plus, the wind has died down." Myrtle waved at Linda, still peering intently at her laptop. "This might be my only opportunity."

Miles sighed. "All right. But I'm only taking a ten-minute walk. You'll need to wrap things up in that time."

"Of course I will."

Miles parked. He stepped out of his sedan, pulling his collar up around his neck. "Ten minutes," he repeated grimly as Myrtle strode toward the coffee shop. It was a modest establishment tucked between a second-hand bookstore and a hardware shop. She stepped in onto worn hardwood floors that creaked under foot. Mismatched tables were scattered about. It wasn't exactly a cozy coffeehouse, but the air was thick with the aroma of freshly ground coffee beans and something sweet baking in the back. A vintage espresso machine hissed and steamed on the counter. The barista was a young woman with vibrant blue hair and multiple piercings. And she didn't talk baby talk to Myrtle as so many young women did. Myrtle appreciated that.

"What can I get for you?" The barista asked briskly, giving Myrtle a smile.

Myrtle knew there was an entire arcane vocabulary for coffee now. But that didn't mean she had to use it. "A large coffee with room for cream, please."

"Coming right up," said the young woman. She set about efficiently to pour it.

Soon Myrtle was walking toward Linda's table. Myrtle cleared her throat, but Linda was too deeply engrossed in her work to look up. Finally, Myrtle decided to simply speak. "Linda? How are you, dear? I haven't seen you since the service."

Chapter Nineteen

Linda started a bit, then smiled. "Hi there, Miss Myrtle. Would you like to join me?"

It was nice to be asked. Far nicer than Nat had behaved. Myrtle disliked feeling as if she was an imposition, even if she was. "That would be lovely, Linda, thank you. Just for a moment—I'll have to meet my friend soon."

"Miles, was it?" asked Linda, looking curious.

"Yes, that's right."

Linda smiled. "You two seem to have a great relationship."

Myrtle laughed, but not unkindly. "Oh, we're just friends. I'm quite a bit older than he is, you know. But we do enjoy hanging out." She took a sip of coffee, then gestured to Linda's notebook. "What inspires your different creations?"

"My designs? Mostly, it's just a matter of delivering what the customer is looking for, in the confines of their vision. So I can't really let my imagination run wild," said Linda with a smile. "Although sometimes I'll draw in my sketchbook, just to let the creative juices start running."

Myrtle said, "Do you? How fascinating. I've always wished had talent in the arts. It just wasn't to be."

"Would you like to see some of my drawings?" asked Linda, perhaps feeling sorry that Myrtle's artistic dreams came to naught.

Myrtle nodded eagerly, and Linda opened the sketchbook.

Myrtle studied them carefully, gently flipping through the pages. She wasn't entirely sure what she was looking at, but she knew they were very good. There were intricate mandalas, geometric patterns spiraling outwards with tiny, precise details. Then there were fanciful drawings of teapots that were tiny houses, a pencil that was a rocket ship. "These are wonderful," she said.

Linda looked pleased as she closed the sketchbook. "Thanks. Sketching for myself is sort of my reward for doing work that's a lot less creative."

Myrtle said, "After we spoke at the service, I ended up looking up your designs online, just out of curiosity. I saw all sorts of things you'd made. You're quite prolific."

"It pays the bills," said Linda. "I do enjoy creating business logos and doing web design. That's a little more creative than coming up with menu designs and that kind of thing." She gave a wistful smile. "Teddy used to challenge me to think beyond conventions. To bring something extra to a project."

"That surprises me," said Myrtle. "From what I'd heard, Teddy favored a traditional approach to his flower arranging. I understood he wasn't as much in favor of Ollie's avant-garde techniques."

"True. But Teddy was a businessman first. He knew how to make money. Teddy realized people buying flowers in the town of Bradley were not looking for off-the-wall, artsy creations.

They wanted simple bouquets. But that doesn't mean Teddy couldn't think outside the box. He'd make flower arrangements for the shop sometimes, and they were totally spectacular." Linda looked reminiscent. Then she sobered. "I heard Curtis Walsh died."

"It's awful, isn't it?"

Linda nodded. "It is. I heard it was at a job site. Do you think it was an accident? I know things happen on these construction sites. Did Red say anything to you about it?" She peered closely at Myrtle as if she could find the answer on her face.

Myrtle said, "Red didn't, but from everything I understand from my reporting, it was murder—no accident."

Linda winced, suddenly looking exhausted. "That's terrible. Who would want to murder Curtis? And he had a young family, too." She paused. "I guess I knew, deep-down, that it wasn't an accident. Red had come over to talk with me yesterday afternoon. I figured he wouldn't be doing that if it was a job incident."

Myrtle nodded. "How did your conversation with Red go?"

"Not great. I told him I'd been working from home early yesterday. Alone, naturally. It's a pity the cat can't give me an alibi."

Myrtle asked, "Did Red ask questions about anything in particular? I'm just curious what angle the police are working."

Linda considered this. "He asked about Nat Drake a little. I told Red what I knew—that Nat owned some property Teddy wanted to save for an endangered salamander." She shrugged. "Nat came over to talk to Teddy about it. And a couple of time

I heard Teddy's end of a phone conversation with him. But it's not like they were at each other's throats or anything. It was all very civilized."

Which was exactly what Nat had said. A business disagreement, he'd called it. "Still, I'd imagine Nat must have been pretty steamed that he wasn't able to develop his own property."

Linda shrugged again. "You win some, you lose some, right? Teddy was pleased at the outcome, of course. He cared about the salamander but also thought the development wasn't good for Bradley. It wasn't something I understood, but I appreciated the fact that he could be so passionate about animals."

Myrtle said, "And the issue with Curtis? Did Red ask about that?"

"Oh, yeah. But it wasn't as if Curtis was threatening to kill Teddy. He was *mad*, don't get me wrong. But he wasn't out for blood."

Myrtle asked, "Did Red bring up Ollie?" She leaned forward as if someone might want to listen in. Although no one was in the shop but the blue-haired woman, who didn't seem remotely interested in overhearing their conversation. "I saw how you were trying to escape him at the service, dear. You left very abruptly."

Linda flushed. "True. I'm worried Ollie may be trying to get back together with me. I've recently found out he had much deeper feelings for me than I realized. For me, dating Ollie just meant I had somebody to go to dinner with or to text with. Something to do. I didn't understand that he felt so strongly about me."

"Has Ollie been in contact with you since Teddy's death?"

Linda sighed. "No. At first, he was avoiding my calls because I believe he knew I wanted to make sure he knew it was over."

"You were trying to reach Ollie?"

"I wanted to make it clear that I wasn't going to get back together with him just because Teddy was out of the picture. Now things have flipped. I'm just about to the point of blocking him on my phone."

Linda looked nervous to Myrtle. She was also glancing away, as if there was something she was purposefully omitting from her narrative. Was Linda trying to divert attention from herself as a suspect?

Miles walked by the window. He looked meaningfully at Myrtle. His face was flushed with the cold.

Myrtle carefully looked away. "Is Ollie harassing you? Should you talk to Red about it?"

"No, no. It's nothing I can't handle. It's just annoying. Ollie doesn't seem to get the message that I'm not interested. You'd think that he'd have given up after I've brushed him off so many times. Instead, it's almost like he thinks that, now that Teddy's out of the picture, maybe I'll get back together with him."

"And that's not the case?"

Linda said, "It couldn't be further from the case."

Myrtle nodded. "The last time we spoke, you mentioned that you thought Zoey might have something to do with Teddy's death. Do you still feel the same?"

"Nothing's changed. Although I can't imagine why she'd want to kill Curtis." Linda frowned. "Unless Curtis saw something incriminating. Maybe he saw Zoey over at the shop before Teddy died. That would definitely be a motive for murdering him." Linda sighed again. "Actually, Zoey showed up at my house the night after the memorial service. I almost didn't let her in. I *wish* I hadn't let her in. She was sloppy drunk and just sad."

"The poor thing," murmured Myrtle. She noticed Miles had left to make another chilly lap around the block.

Linda said, "You know, I struggle to feel sorry for her. I mean, I *do* feel sorry to a certain extent. I understand addiction to alcohol is tough, and it's like any other chronic illness. But Zoey seems to be her own worst enemy in so many other ways, too. She can't hold down a job, is terrible with family relationships, and can't get a grip on her finances. I mostly felt bad for Teddy, who had to deal with her."

"Why did Zoey decide to come over to talk to you?"

Linda said, "Because she'd been drinking. But her excuse was that she didn't have any recent photos of Teddy. She wanted me to share some with her." She rolled her eyes. "To me, it really said something that his own sister didn't have pictures of him. That's because she thinks of herself all the time. Not anybody else."

Myrtle said quietly, "It's amazing you still had pictures of Teddy. I'd have thought you might have wanted to delete them after he unceremoniously broke up with you."

Linda looked startled, then looked down at her coffee. "You figured that out, did you?" She took a big sip of her coffee. "Yeah, he did. Not long before he died. I guess I just didn't want to admit it had happened. I was in denial." She laughed darkly. "Now I'm starting to sound like Ollie. That's a clue I need to get over this."

Myrtle said, "You know how relationships are. You and Teddy might have been back together a week later."

"We'll never know, will we?" asked Linda sadly.

Miles walked slowly by the window again. This time, he looked blue instead of flushed. "There's my friend. Good seeing you, Linda. Hope things start looking up."

"Thanks, Miss Myrtle."

"Heavens, Miles, do we need to defrost you?"

Miles said, "It's colder than it looks out here."

"I suppose that's seasonal. It's February, after all."

Miles turned up the heat in his car and put his hands in front of the vent. "How did things go with Linda?"

"She was a bit more forthcoming this time, although I do still wonder if she's telling the whole truth. She admitted that the breakup from Ollie was not an easy one. And it appears Ollie may have had feelings for Linda."

Miles said, "So Ollie might have wanted to get Teddy out of the way and clear his path back to Linda."

"Perhaps. The only problem with that scenario is Teddy broke up with Linda. Linda admitted it, and we've heard it from Perkins, too. So why would Ollie feel the need to murder Teddy to end up with Linda?"

Miles said, "For revenge? Not just for stealing Ollie's girlfriend, but also for firing him."

"True. But Linda had her grievances with Teddy, too. She was abruptly dumped. Hitting someone on the head with a nearby vase could certainly indicate a crime of passion. A spur-of-the-moment murder. Maybe she went back over to try to talk things out with Teddy, and he rejected Linda again. It's something to think about, at least." Myrtle glanced at her watch. "Would you look at that? It's actually a decent time of the morning now. Shops are opening up. And the library."

Miles was now very good at reading between the lines when it came to Myrtle. "You're wanting to go to the library."

"Do you mind? I need to find myself something to read. Something for those middle-of-the-night hours."

Miles asked, "Does that mean boring books? Books to help you fall asleep?"

"Books don't seem to do that for me, somehow. I don't find them lulling. If they *are* lulling, I'm reading the wrong book. So, no, I believe I'll look for a medical thriller or a haunted house story. Something entertaining."

Miles said, "The only problem is my upcoming dental appointment. I got a reminder text while I was walking around the block. And around the block."

Myrtle frowned. "What does that have to do with book selection?"

"Nothing. But it has quite a lot to do with taking you to the library. How long exactly are you wanting to stay there?"

Myrtle said, "I have no idea. It will likely take me a while to browse through the books. The Bradley library has a fairly extensive collection, you know. Why don't you just drop me off, and I'll walk home?'"

"But you'll be carrying books with you. How will you manage books with your cane?"

Myrtle said, "The librarians always give me a bag to tote my books in. It's really no problem at all, Miles. Go get your teeth cleaned."

Miles started driving toward the library. "I could always reschedule."

"You're not using me as an excuse to get out of the appointment."

Myrtle walked into the library and over to the new books section. The old books section was also fine, but she'd read so many of the offerings that she'd often end up in a situation where she thought she hadn't read a book, but then found later that she had. Then the ending would be ruined. Sticking with new books was definitely the safer approach.

One librarian was familiar with both Myrtle and her reading habits. She recommended a couple of books for her. Then Myrtle was on her way, a lot sooner than she'd thought she might be. She supposed Miles could have waited for her after all. Still, she didn't mind a walk home. It wasn't nearly as chilly as it had been when Miles was out earlier.

Myrtle was walking past the coffee shop on the way home when she saw Linda climbing into a rather distinctive-looking car. It jogged something in her brain. She paused on the sidewalk to figure out where she'd seen the car before. Then she remembered. It had passed them going away from the construction site where Curtis Walsh's body had been found. Why had Linda been over there?

Myrtle tried calling Miles, thinking he might not have gotten to his appointment yet. Or that he'd scrapped the dental cleaning altogether since he hadn't sounded at all enthusiastic about it. But his phone went straight to voice mail, so he must have done the right thing and headed over there.

She suddenly felt as if she should follow Linda and have another word with her. However, Myrtle didn't do dumb things. She felt very scornful toward women in books and on film who deliberately did dangerous things that put them in horrible circumstances. Investigating strange noises in a dark basement or splitting up from a group to explore a creepy, abandoned house alone. So she called Wanda.

Wanda picked up right away. "I'm comin'," she said grimly.

"Are you? Splendid! I was hoping to follow Linda to her house, but there's no way for you to get here in time. Maybe we can drive around and look for her distinctive car. Thankfully, it's not a large town."

Wanda was quiet for a moment. "221C Lakefront Drive."

"Heavens, Wanda! The Sight has truly been unbelievable lately."

"No Sight. Jest th' internet," said the psychic.

"Ah. I'm surprised you could find her address so quickly."

Wanda said, "Does her work outta her house, so it came right up."

"Oh, right. That makes sense. Okay, well, be careful driving over, Wanda. I'll meet you at my house."

Wanda had definitely heeded Myrtle's warning to drive carefully. She took her time on the way over. It was fine because Myrtle realized she wanted to pick up a couple of things at the grocery store on the way home. And, perhaps, she needed time to formulate a good excuse to visit Linda. After all, they'd just enjoyed a cup of coffee together that very morning. And, even with the protection of Wanda at her side, she felt she might need to be especially cautious.

Myrtle hurried into the Piggly Wiggly, stopped by the clearance aisle, then hurried back out again and back home. When she saw Wanda's car pull into the driveway, she grabbed one of the baguettes Elaine had so kindly provided her with.

When Myrtle walked out to the car with the bread, Wanda gave her a wry look. "That could kill somebody."

"Or maim them. I'd like to keep my possibilities open. This could be a very dangerous woman."

Wanda set off slowly down the road. "Or not. Mebbe she's not."

"Do you have any of your special insights that you need to share?"

Wanda shook her head.

"What about the earlier insight? The one about habits?" Myrtle frowned in recollection.

"Don't got more info on it."

But Myrtle's memory was jogged once again. "On the way to Linda's, can we drive by Ollie's house? Just so I can check something."

Myrtle directed Wanda to Ollie's. There she saw no boot and no car. His dirty boots hadn't been there when she'd spoken with him yesterday, either. Had Ollie set out on his daily stroll by the lake a bit later than usual? Or was he wearing his grubby boots in his car?

Wanda, who'd slowed her already-sluggish acceleration down to five miles per hour, asked, "Want me to make a second pass?"

"No, I think I'm good," said Myrtle, sounding distracted.

Wanda hazarded a look at her friend. "Everythin' okay?"

"I don't think so. Thinking of a change of habit made me consider Ollie. I've been ruminating on the fact that Ollie really shouldn't put his gross boots on the front porch when it functions as his place of business."

Wanda nodded. "He takes them walks by the lake. An' in the woods."

"Precisely. Then he's home by nine a.m., takes the grubby boots off, puts them by the front door, and goes in to get started with his workday. But now there's been a change. So is Ollie out in his car right now? It's after nine. And is he wearing those awful boots?"

Wanda stole another quick glance at Myrtle. "Or did he wear them boots yestiddy?"

"And were the boots covered in blood and Curtis Walsh's DNA? Are the boots now at the bottom of the lake? Or in a landfill?" Myrtle scowled at the thought.

Wanda said, "So are we still gonna see Linda? Or are we gonna wait fer Ollie?"

"The problem is I saw Linda's car leaving the construction site," said Myrtle slowly. "Yesterday morning, that is. So, did Linda have to kill Curtis because he knew she murdered Teddy? Or was Linda over at the site for another reason altogether?"

Wanda swallowed. "Like she followed Ollie? Like she wanted to talk to 'im?"

"Exactly like that. Let's go see Linda."

Chapter Twenty

The Oakwood Apartments on Lakefront Drive is a three-story brick building from the 1970s, situated on a quiet, tree-lined street. Its faded yellow siding and dark green trim gave it a slightly dated but homey appearance. The apartments seemed to be accessible via external staircases and open-air walkways.

"There's Linda's car," said Myrtle, pointing to an older model Volkswagen Beetle in a metallic green color. "She must be here."

They walked up to 221C. Linda came quickly to the door opening it just a crack. She opened it wider when she saw Myrtle there. "Miss Myrtle!" she said, startled. Linda looked even more startled when she spotted Wanda. Wanda gave her a kind, gap toothed grin.

Myrtle said, "I'm so sorry to bother you, dear. This is my friend, Wanda. There's something I realized just a few minutes ago. Do you mind if I come in?"

Linda hesitated. "I'm really sorry, but I'm in the middle of a project."

"Oh, it'll just take a minute. Also, I hope you don't mind, but I think I should borrow your restroom. All that coffee from earlier, you know."

Now Linda opened the door. "Of course. Coffee runs right through me, too. It's through that door and to the right."

Myrtle walked in. "You have a lovely place! And so neat and clean."

"Since I work from home, I try to stay on top of the mess. I have a cleaning lady."

Myrtle gave Linda's immaculate baseboards a sour look. "That's right. Bitsy cleans for you. I use her cousin, Puddin."

"Is Puddin any good?" asked Linda.

"I wouldn't recommend her." Myrtle headed in the direction of the bathroom, laying down the baguette on a narrow table in the hallway as she did.

Wanda slowly walked in, looking apologetically at Linda. "Sorry," she mumbled.

"No, it's just fine. I totally understand."

Wanda said, "I'll jest wait back there for Myrtle. Let yew git 'er stuff done."

Linda gave her a distracted nod, already looking toward her computer. "Thanks. I was just going to send this email real quick."

Wanda slipped into the back of the apartment, waiting for Myrtle. She put her arms around herself. Myrtle came out of the bathroom. "At least I got us inside," said Myrtle quietly. She frowned, looking at Wanda. "What's wrong?"

Wanda held out her arm. There were goosebumps up and down it. From Wanda's expression, Myrtle could tell it wasn't a good sign.

"What are we doing hiding in the back hallway?" asked Myrtle in a whisper.

"Jest wait," said Wanda. She turned, looking stoically toward the living room.

They didn't have to wait long. Myrtle and Wanda could hear Linda's front door come flying open.

"Ollie," they heard Linda gasp. "What are you doing here?"

"What am I doing here? What do you think? I saw you driving away yesterday morning from the construction site. I've been trying to track you down since then. You thought you could just ignore me? Not answer the door? Or my phone calls?"

Myrtle thought Ollie must be singularly bad at tracking Linda. Myrtle herself had found her only this morning at the coffee shop. She glanced over at Wanda, who was wordlessly watching, her eyes gleaming.

"Get out of here," said Linda. "I mean it. Get out!"

Myrtle had already dialed 9-1-1. Then she turned on her voice recorder. At the very least, the police could arrest Ollie for trespassing. Or perhaps stalking. But she was very much hoping Ollie might say something to incriminate himself.

"You saw me at the construction site yesterday. I saw your car pull in."

Linda's voice was shaking. "I didn't see anything."

"Really? You seemed to stick around a long time for someone who didn't see anything."

Linda said, "I was just waiting to talk to you."

"And you couldn't answer the phone the last twenty-four hours?" scoffed Ollie.

"I wanted to talk to you *before* the last twenty-four hours."

Ollie's voice was ominous. "So what changed? Let me guess. You saw something at the construction site. You saw I had to get rid of Curtis Walsh. And now I have to get rid of you. Which was the last thing I wanted to do."

Myrtle and Wanda looked at each other. Then Wanda took a deep breath and sprang out of the hallway hiding place into the kitchen. "Hi there," she said softly.

Chapter Twenty-One

Ollie gaped at the sight of the skin-and-bones psychic. He muttered something disbelieving under his breath, then lurched for Wanda, a knife in his hand. Which was when Myrtle, who'd retrieved Elaine's cast-iron baguette from the narrow table, smacked Ollie as hard over the head as she possibly could.

Ollie dropped to the floor, stunned. But not stunned enough for Myrtle, who struck him again until the knife came flying out of his hand, skittering across the kitchen floor. Now Ollie was still.

Linda stared at his motionless figure, her face white. Wanda grabbed a napkin to pick up the knife, then walked to the far corner of the apartment with it. Myrtle had her phone out and was briskly calling Red. "It's me. I've got your killer for you. 221C Lakefront Drive. He's been immobilized." She listened for a moment, then said crossly, "Yes, he's alive. Now get over here."

Myrtle did check for a pulse, just to make absolutely sure Ollie was indeed alive. He was lying so very still, and Elaine's bread was quite lethal in its density. Fortunately, there was a pulse, and Myrtle could retreat.

Linda took a shaky breath. "Thanks. Thanks so much, you two."

Myrtle gave her a smile. "Would you like a glass of water, dear? You're looking rather peaked. Or perhaps a cracker or something?"

Linda sank down in a kitchen chair, shaking her head. "No. No, I'm all right."

"Okay. So, before my son comes barreling in here like the Lone Ranger, let's talk for a minute. Why were you over at the construction site where Curtis Walsh was murdered yesterday?"

Linda said, "I wanted to talk to Ollie and tell him it was over. I think he knew I was trying to reach him to make sure he understood. He hadn't been answering his phone or even his door when I went by his house. I dropped by yesterday morning, early, hoping to catch Ollie off-guard and make sure we were on the same page."

Myrtle said, "But he was leaving his house when you arrived?"

"That's right. So I decided to follow Ollie. I didn't understand what he was doing over at a construction site, but I parked the car and headed over to talk to him."

Myrtle frowned. "That doesn't sound like a very safe approach. It was early in the morning. Hardly anyone was around. Ollie could have lashed out at you for the rejection. And, as far as you knew, he could have been a killer. In fact, he *was* a killer."

Linda said, "I was trying to be careful. I had one of those big metal flashlights with me—the kind the police carry. I had running shoes on. I was carrying my phone in my hand with 11 pulled up, just in case." She shrugged. "But yes, it still wasn't smart. I think I was lulled into a sense of safety because I *knew* Ollie. Because we'd dated. I thought I knew him better than I did." She looked over at the man on the floor, disbelief still etched on her features.

Sirens were approaching. Myrtle was still gripping her baguette in case Ollie started moving about.

"What did you see?" she asked.

Linda took a deep breath. "Nothing. But I put two-and-two together later. I walked up to the site. There was another car there, but I figured somebody might be working on a different point of the property, and I could still have a quiet moment with Ollie."

Wanda's eyes were fixed on Linda. "He were arguin' with somebody."

"Exactly," said Linda. "Ollie was having an argument with another man. I figured it wouldn't be a good time to have that talk with him. I turned around and headed back to my car."

"How did Ollie realize you were there at all?" asked Myrtle.

Linda said slowly, "A lot of things happened at one time. A truck drove up."

"That must have been Hank, one of the construction workers," said Myrtle with a nod.

"He sat in his truck for a few minutes, looking at his phone. Then I saw Ollie coming out of the side of the construction."

"Could Hank see him?" asked Myrtle.

Linda shook her head. "No. Ollie had parked on the other side of the building from Hank. Besides, Hank was totally absorbed in his phone."

The sirens stopped in front of the apartment building. Ollie groaned on the floor and opened an eye. Myrtle brandished the loaf at him, and he closed it again.

A second later, Red pounded on the door, then opened it. EMTs were right behind him. Behind *them* was Lieutenant Perkins.

"Is everybody okay?" Red demanded.

"*He's* not," said Myrtle, gesturing at Ollie with the loaf.

"Is that . . . Elaine's bread?"

Myrtle nodded. "You'll have to tell her she made some really excellent bread."

"I won't encourage her," muttered Red. He watched as the EMTs examined Ollie, then carefully removed him. "Possible concussion," explained one of them.

Red shook his head, watching as Ollie was taken out of the apartment. "Okay, so everybody tell me what is going on, please."

No one seemed to know where to start.

Perkins asked, "Miss Lambert?"

Linda gave a quick recap of what she'd told Myrtle and Wanda. She cleared her throat. "So, like I was saying earlier, Ollie left the building, unseen by Hank. Hank was then getting out of his truck. I started to drive away, but Ollie spotted me."

Red said, "You weren't interested in talking to Ollie anymore?"

"Well, I'd heard him arguing. That told me he was already in foul mood. It didn't seem like the right time to have a conversation with him."

Myrtle said, "Miles and I saw you on your way out."

It was news to Red that his mother had been at the construction site. "You *what*?"

Myrtle gave him a regal look. "Miles and I were on our way to get breakfast when we saw all the emergency vehicles. We couldn't help but investigate."

Red rubbed his forehead as if it had also been smacked by Elaine's baguette.

Linda said, "Yes, I remember seeing a car approaching when I was leaving. That was you, then?"

Myrtle nodded. "But we didn't see Ollie leaving."

Linda said, "He was heading out a back entrance in the other direction."

Red took out his notebook. "Okay, let me recap this because there's a lot of coming and going in this retelling."

"*I* follow it," said Myrtle. She looked for opportunities to showcase her superior cognitive ability.

Red ignored her interjection. "So, Linda, you followed Ollie to tell him to back off. He'd been ignoring your calls because he wanted to continue believing you might get back together."

Linda nodded.

"When you got to the site, Ollie was already arguing with somebody. You decided to leave. Hank, a construction worker arrived on the scene but didn't approach until after Ollie had already walked out of the site."

Linda nodded again. Myrtle sighed in a bored manner.

"Then you left. You saw my mom, who was driving toward the site."

Another nod.

Lt. Perkins added, "And Ollie drove away in another direction."

Linda said, "That's right." She picked up with her narrative. "I headed back home to get some work done. I figured I'd try to get in touch with Ollie again after he'd had a chance to cool down. But then I heard about Curtis Walsh's death. And where his death occurred."

Perkins said, "And you knew Ollie must have been the killer."

Red narrowed his eyes. "But you didn't contact the police department."

Linda was apparently worried she was going to be implicated as an accessory in some way. She quickly said, "I wanted to. I picked up the phone half a dozen times to make that call. But I didn't see or hear anything incriminating."

Red raised his eyebrows. "You saw Ollie Spearman at the scene of the crime. You knew he would be a major suspect." He paused. "We'll let that go for now. Tell me what the last day has been like."

Linda looked pale again. "As soon as I found out Curtis was murdered, I knew I wanted to avoid Ollie. The thing was, he kept trying to reach out."

"Where he was avoiding you before," said Red.

Linda nodded. "But I thought I knew why he wanted to reach out. Because he must have spotted my car as I was leaving. I have a metallic green Beetle, so it really stands out. But I wasn't answering his calls or texts." She looked at Myrtle. "I did go out this morning to the coffeehouse to clear my head, but I went to a public spot so nothing would happen to me. I needed to think, absorb the news about Curtis. Figure out what I should do next."

Myrtle said, "You did seem to have a lot on your mind this morning."

Red rolled his eyes at further evidence of his mother's meddling.

Linda looked at Red. "Because Ollie was desperate and couldn't get in touch with me, he came over here. He barged in because the door was unlocked. I don't know if he'll confess or not, but Wanda and Miss Myrtle both heard him threaten me."

"I have his threats on my phone," said Myrtle, holding up the device. Perkins gave her an approving smile.

"Of course you do," said Red in a tired voice. He added, "The witness testimony and the digital evidence will definitely help. Mama, I'll send a cop over later to collect the evidence from your phone. But there were also fibers taken at Teddy Hartfield's crime scene. After the labs run some DNA, I'm hopeful there will be a match."

Myrtle's phone chimed. She glanced at it to find Miles had just texted her. She looked over at Wanda. "Miles is done at the dentist and wants an update."

Wanda gave her a weary grin. "We gotta big update."

"Indeed, we do. Perhaps we should set out on our way."

Red said, "I think that's a wonderful idea."

"Good seeing you, Mrs. Clover. You too, Wanda," said Perkins politely.

Linda reached out to give them both a hug. In a teary voice she said, "Thanks for saving my life."

Wanda drove them away from the apartment building. Myrtle said, "Let's go to my house. Can you visit for a while? We should celebrate solving the case. With Miles, of course. Although he was at the dentist during the final bit."

"Sure thing," said Wanda, inching her car in that direction.

Myrtle said, "You were right, as always, you know. Ollie changed his habit of putting his muddy boots on his front porch before starting work. Who knows what he did with those boots after leaving the construction site?"

"Reckon he threw 'em out."

"Perhaps in a landfill. I suppose they had evidence on them from the scene of the crime. Hopefully Red and his gang can locate them and use them in court," said Myrtle. She looked out the car window at the slowly moving scenery. "It's a pity Curtis found it necessary to blackmail Ollie. At least, I suppose that's why Curtis was meeting with Ollie at the construction site. If he'd only told the police what he saw instead of telling Ollie, he might still be alive."

Wanda stopped at a stop sign, put her blinker on, and sat watchfully for a few moments before turning left. "Yep. Shoulda just told the cops."

Myrtle said, "Ollie always was a good suspect, of course. He had plenty of reason to want Teddy out of the way. It was all about revenge, wasn't it? Revenge for Teddy firing him, revenge for Teddy stealing Linda away from him."

"Don't think Linda an' Ollie woulda been together long anyway," noted Wanda.

"No, I suppose not. Linda seems like a very independent woman. She owns a business, she maintains her own home. She really didn't need a clingy man like Ollie appeared to be." Myrtle frowned. "It seems like I'm forgetting something important. What can that be?"

"Mebbe that article on Ollie?"

Myrtle snapped her fingers. "You're right! I'll call Sloan and tell him to stop the presses. I've always wanted to say that. The *Bradley Bugle* certainly doesn't need to be running a fawning feature on Ollie Spearman and his floral business. Now, I have a completely different story in mind."

A few minutes later, Wanda pulled into Myrtle's driveway. Wanda said, "Think Erma is on her way over."

Myrtle made a face. "I simply can't be dealing with Erma right now. It's completely impossible. I swear the woman lies in wait for me like a spider in a web."

Wanda stepped out of the car, made a clicking noise, and Pasha came bounding up. Pasha adored Wanda, and the feeling was mutual. Pasha was much less fond of Erma, and the feeling was also mutual there. Erma made an abrupt about-face and headed back toward her own house, much to Myrtle's relief.

Myrtle took out her phone and texted Miles back. "I'm asking Miles to come on over. I said we had news. That should tempt him."

Sure enough, a minute later, Miles was knocking on the door. Wanda let him in, grinning at him.

"What's up?" asked Miles.

"Wanda and I solved the case," said Myrtle smugly.

Miles's eyes opened wide. "What happened?" he demanded.

They filled him in. Wanda's prediction, Myrtle's observant nature, Ollie's boots, and a visit to see Linda.

"And you knocked Ollie out with Elaine's bread?" asked Miles.

"That I did. It proved a formidable weapon, in the right hands. And now, enough of murder and mayhem for a few minutes." Myrtle delved into a kitchen cabinet, where she pulled out a small bag. "Sweets to the sweet."

She dumped the bag on the kitchen table, rather like a child with a Halloween haul. There were heart-shaped chocolates wrapped in foil. Lots of them.

"We're going to eat chocolates until we pop at the seams," stated Myrtle, sounding very pleased with herself.

"You bought a lot of Valentine candy," said Miles, staring at the pile.

"It was on sale. Greatly reduced. Their loss, our gain."

"Any updates on the copyediting situation?" asked Miles.

"Yew git th' job?" asked Wanda.

Myrtle nodded, pleased with herself. "Yes indeedy. The copyediting job is open, and I'm sure Sloan will give it to me when I ask for it. Imogen Winthrop wisely gave up her position."

"Was it Elaine's bread that discouraged Imogen?" asked Miles. "I'd imagine that would be the final straw."

"I'll hear nothing against Elaine's bread. After all, it saved our lives today. As far as Imogen goes, the job was simply too much for her," said Myrtle with a shrug. "I always knew she'd crack under pressure."

Wanda had already started pulling foil off several of the candies. Soon the three friends were eating chocolates, drinking glasses of milk, and watching *Tomorrow's Promise* together. As the familiar theme song played, Myrtle looked around at her friends, the pile of chocolates, and her cozy living room. She smiled contentedly, thinking that sometimes the sweetest mysteries in life were the ones shared with good company and even better desserts.

About the Author

Bestselling cozy mystery author Elizabeth Spann Craig is a library-loving, avid mystery reader. A pet-owning Southerner, her four series are full of cats, corgis, and cheese grits. The mother of two, she lives with her husband, a fun-loving corgi, and a couple of cute cats.

Sign up for Elizabeth's free newsletter to stay updated on releases:

https://bit.ly/2xZUXqO

This and That

I love hearing from my readers. You can find me on Facebook as Elizabeth Spann Craig Author, on Twitter as elizabethscraig, on my website at elizabethspanncraig.com, and by email at elizabethspanncraig@gmail.com.

Thanks so much for reading my book...I appreciate it. If you enjoyed the story, would you please leave a short review on the site where you purchased it? Just a few words would be great. Not only do I feel encouraged reading them, but they also help other readers discover my books. Thank you!

Did you know my books are available in print and ebook formats? Most of the Myrtle Clover series is available in audio and some of the Southern Quilting mysteries are. Find the audiobooks here: https://elizabethspanncraig.com/audio/

Please follow me on BookBub for my reading recommendations and release notifications.

I'd also like to thank some folks who helped me put this book together. A special thanks to Rebecca Wahr and her daughter and Cassie Kelley for storyline help for *Mystery Love Company*.

Thanks to my cover designer, Karri Klawiter, for her awesome covers. Thanks to my editor, Judy Beatty for her help. Thanks to beta readers Amanda Arrieta, Rebecca Wahr, Cassie Kelley, and Dan Harris for all of their helpful suggestions and careful reading. Thanks to my ARC readers for helping to spread the word. Thanks, as always, to my family and readers.

Other Works by Elizabeth

Myrtle Clover Series in Order (be sure to look for the Myrtle series in audio, ebook, and print):

Pretty is as Pretty Dies

Progressive Dinner Deadly

A Dyeing Shame

A Body in the Backyard

Death at a Drop-In

A Body at Book Club

Death Pays a Visit

A Body at Bunco

Murder on Opening Night

Cruising for Murder

Cooking is Murder

A Body in the Trunk

Cleaning is Murder

Edit to Death

Hushed Up

A Body in the Attic

Murder on the Ballot

Death of a Suitor

A Dash of Murder
Death at a Diner
A Myrtle Clover Christmas
Murder at a Yard Sale
Doom and Bloom
A Toast to Murder
Mystery Loves Company (2025)

THE VILLAGE LIBRARY Mysteries in Order:
Checked Out
Overdue
Borrowed Time
Hush-Hush
Where There's a Will
Frictional Characters
Spine Tingling
A Novel Idea
End of Story
Booked Up
Out of Circulation
Shelf Life (2025)
The Sunset Ridge Mysteries in Order
The Type-A Guide to Solving Murder
The Type-A Guide to Dinner Parties (2025)
Southern Quilting Mysteries in Order:
Quilt or Innocence
Knot What it Seams

Quilt Trip
Shear Trouble
Tying the Knot
Patch of Trouble
Fall to Pieces
Rest in Pieces
On Pins and Needles
Fit to be Tied
Embroidering the Truth
Knot a Clue
Quilt-Ridden
Needled to Death
A Notion to Murder
Crosspatch
Behind the Seams
Quilt Complex
A Southern Quilting Cozy Christmas

MEMPHIS BARBEQUE MYSTERIES in Order (Written as Riley Adams):
Delicious and Suspicious
Finger Lickin' Dead
Hickory Smoked Homicide
Rubbed Out
And a standalone "cozy zombie" novel: Race to Refuge written as Liz Craig

Made in United States
Orlando, FL
13 September 2024

51470456R00122